In Praise

Riveting! A compelling, amazing, enjoyable, and exciting romance. Debra –**Amazon Reviewer**

Holy Hotness!! Conor Murphy is one sexy badass Irishman who had his eyes set on Ava Jackson from the get-go. Ms. London really knows how to take her readers down the rabbit hole! -**Author Daisy St. James**

This book was gripping, well-written & the chemistry between the characters, Conor & Ava, sizzled throughout this wonderful read. Libby –**Booksprout Reviewer**

This book grabs you at the first word and doesn't let go till the very satisfying end. The characters and chemistry they share is just awesome! Katherine–**Goodreads Reviewer**

CASSIDY LONDON

Freefall

International Love 1

Cassidy London

www.cassidylondon.com

CASSIDY LONDON

ISBN: 978-1-7773017-0-5

Other Books by

CASSIDY LONDON

NEW ADULT ROMANCE TRILOGY
INTERNATIONAL LOVE SERIES

Freefall (#1) -Forbidden Love
Layover (#2) -Second Chance
Heatwave (#3) -Secret Billionaire

ENEMIES TO LOVERS
STAND ALONE
Inked Love

SWINGERS ROMANCE NOVELLAS
SUBURBAN SECRETS SERIES

Couples Night Out (#1)
Weekend Getaway (#2)
Island Resort (#3)

CASSIDY LONDON

For Alix.
Here's to pulling the alternator every damn day.

CASSIDY LONDON

Freefall

International Love 1

Chapter 1

New York, JFK Airport

Ava Jackson

"I would totally fuck him." Sighed Adriana as she stared lustfully at an image of Jason Momoa plastered on a cover of the latest issue of People magazine. "Maybe I'll find a guy like that this summer…" She continued wistfully staring off into the glossy pages.

"In your dreams girl!" Samantha giggled as she scoured through the pages of another magazine. "Jason's not bad, but honestly, no one does it for me like Adam." Referring to Adam Levine, she bumped hips with Adriana, practically knocking her over into the candy display.

Watching my friends made me smile and chuckle to myself. This would be one hell of a crazy summer. College was finally over, and we were all dying to let loose and explore the world. This trip was all we'd been talking about for months now. Truth was, most of our senior year had been about planning this European tour.

Out of the three of us, Adriana was the only one who had been to Europe before. Her family was originally from Portugal. She had been born in Lisbon, and had gone home to visit family many times. She'd also toured around a bunch of European countries over the years. For her, Europe was like coming home. But for Sam and I, well… we had stars in our eyes and it filled us with every possible romanticized idea of what Europe would be like.

Turning, Sam asked, "What about you, Ava?"

"Yeah, who's your celebrity crush of the moment?" Adriana chimed in.

"Girls. I have no time for celebrity crushes. I'm looking for a real man." I winked, sending them into a fit of giggles. "And, seeing as we will all be wandering around Europe all summer, I'm hoping that I'll have at least two or three options in each country." I finished, popping my tongue out at them.

"Yass! Finally!" Sam yelled, slapping me on the back. "We've been waiting for you to get with the program for years, Ava!"

A sheepish smile crossed my lips as I rolled my eyes at them. I'd known for a while now that it was time to move on and forget the past. The mantra my therapist had taught me played repeatedly in my head.

Hatred and anger only poisons the person who carries it in their heart.

It had taken a long time to learn to forgive, though.

First, my parents. Then Ryan. And finally, Ashton. At twenty-two years old, I felt like I'd spent most of my life feeling betrayed. But finally, I was ready. Now all I needed were my best friends by my side as we partied it up across Europe. And, a foreign fling or two to make it a little sweeter.

***

Our trip was starting in just twenty-four hours and I could not have been more excited. We had two back-to-back organized tours waiting to take us all over the continent. The first was starting with a tour of the UK and Ireland. Then we had ten days on our own before meeting up with tour number two, which would take us from Paris to Greece.

The many months of planning was all worth it because it would be the absolute best summer of our lives. I'd been dreaming about sunbathing in the Greek Isles just as much as touring the castles and cliffs of Ireland. The Eiffel tower in Paris, to wine tasting in Tuscany. Nothing had been forgotten.

The girls and I had been roommates and best friends since our freshman year at NYU. We had always wanted to take a huge trip together. But other than a few weekends to the shore, and one drunken spring break trip to the Dominican Republic, we had never made it work. We all had family responsibilities that took us back to our respective hometowns during the holidays. We had filled previous summers with internships, summer jobs, and research papers for extra credit. But this was our moment, and what better place to celebrate than Europe?

We ended up buying magazines, candy, and a bunch of other crap we didn't need. "So much for not having a carry-on!" grumbled Sam as she struggled under the weight of four shopping bags as we exited the overpriced convenience store. I had to agree. I had mugs, books, magazines, snacks, and we hadn't even left New York yet. A classy woman's voice echoed throughout the airport:

"British Airways Flight 756 to Dublin–Gate G5... Boarding will begin in five minutes. Five minutes to boarding."

The announcement made the three of us let out simultaneous high-pitched screams as we picked up speed and ran like crazy to our gate. "C'mon! Let's go!" I shouted to my friends. "Shit!" cried out Adri as we ran. "We're fucked if we miss this flight!"

We turned a corner and thankfully, there it was. Gate G5. Fortunately, there was a massive lineup to give us a chance to collect ourselves. Thank goodness.

I slowed my pace and called out to my friends who were still behind me. "Girls! No worries! If there's a lineup, then they're still boarding. We're fine!" Turns out they couldn't hear me through the hustle and bustle of the airport though. I turned and tried again but they ran past me calling "Ava! C'mon!" I followed behind, but at my pace. Not only was it obvious that we would not miss boarding, but there was also no way I could continue to run pulling along the ridiculous amount of hand-held baggage I was lugging.

My dad had insisted that I take a carry-on just in case my luggage got lost. So, my stupid shopping bags on top of a carry-on, and my running, had come to a full stop.

I watched as Samantha and Adriana kept running. They seemed to talk to each other as they went. The lineup was getting closer, but they continued to run blindly forward as they tried to readjust their bags, sweaters, and phones.

And then, before it even happened, I saw the crash. I called out to them one more time to slow down, but it was too late. In a split second, I watched as Adri and Sam collided head-first into a human wall.

Shopping bags, magazines, and purses went flying. Lipstick and a hand cream were rolling away as I approached a few steps behind them. I opened my mouth to ask why they were just standing there while their things rolled away when I saw what they were staring at.

An immense giant-of-a-man with piercing green eyes that seemed to glow turned around. His face was fearsome and expressionless, except for a hint of anger behind his eyes. A full beard accentuated his sculpted cheekbones. Small creases in the corners of his eyes suggested that he was much older than we were. His imposing stance and chiseled build screamed "sex on a stick". I wondered how old he might be. Thirty-five? Maybe even forty? I wasn't sure, but what I knew was that my friends and I were standing with our mouths gaping open in the worst possible way.

He seemed to be staring too, and I wondered why it felt like he was only focused on me. Something caught me in that green gaze. Endless emerald pools were sucking me in, deeper and deeper. He had dirty blond hair, somewhat shaggy on top, that fell across his face in strands and creating a little mystery about him. The way he was not carefully groomed made him even more appealing. He sported a fitted, heather-grey, V-neck t-shirt, revealing tattoos around his collarbone and forearms. Low-slung jeans that seemed to melt onto his hips showed off that he was as fit below the waist as he was above it. Well worn-in combat boots finished his look, confirming that this was not a man you could easily mess with. He was intimidating in the sort of way when you feel an intense attraction to someone and it makes you shy…

A raspy Irish accent finally broke the silence. "You

ladies alright?"

Sam and Adri stammered apologies and giggled as they bent down to clean up the mess they had made. I stood still, frozen in place. I knew I needed to help my friends, but I couldn't move. As he addressed my friends, his eyes never moved from mine. That striking deep green was almost unnatural, but so captivating. He spoke, but he never looked away. Never released his hold on me. I was aware of everything around me, yet I couldn't seem to move a muscle. My friends were still apologizing profusely, but he didn't seem to notice. Finally, when they had gathered all their belongings, they tugged at my arm to join them a few steps back. That's when he turned around, walked out of the line, and briskly up to the gate. We watched as he spoke with the flight attendant. Her stance changed slightly from my perspective. I watched her flipping her hair nervously, as Mr. Green Eye's passport and boarding pass slipped from her hands onto the floor. Her sudden clumsiness derived clearly from the man before her. He seemed to make everyone nervous. She had to bend down carefully as her skirt rose up her thighs and she balanced on her pumps, knees bent together. She managed to stand herself up, apologize, and send him through. I continued watching her as she tried smoothing her uniform and looked completely frazzled. Was everyone under his spell?

"Well, that was fucking crazy!" giggled Sam. "Did you

see that guy? Shit, he was kind of old but still- so fucking hot!" Adri fanned herself dramatically. "A silver fox!" babbled Sam. "Nah… I don't think he was that old." Adri answered.

"What do you think Ava? Ava? Earth to Ava?" Sam shook me from my trance. "Uh sorry…" I stammered. I was so flustered I could barely think, let alone speak.

"OMG… you have it bad for that dude!" Adriana teased. "We haven't even boarded the plane yet, let alone arrived on the other side of the pond!" She continued. "And secondly girlfriend… he was way too old for you!"

"Agreed!" chuckled Samantha as she flipped her perfectly straight blond hair over her shoulder.

"Anyway, with that accent, he was going home. And based on his appearance, he was probably going home to an equally hot wife." Sam continued.

"And, we're going on a vacation to find guys our own age. So enough about that. Let's get on this plane!" Adriana announced as the line diminished and we moved closer to the gate.

We pulled out our passports and boarding passes as we approached the desk. The flight attendant smiled sweetly at us. "Enjoy Ireland girls!"

"We will, thank you!" We cried in unison as we entered

the walkway corridor to the plane.

"Imagine if one of us is seated next to that hot Irishman on the plane?" Sam whispered low enough for Adriana and I to hear. Adri just laughed and shook her head, but I just about choked on the thought. *OMG– that could not happen. I would not make it through an overnight flight next to that man.*

Fortunately, we had three seats together all in a row. I fully had to admit that I looked for him, though. As we walked through first class, I scanned the rows of people putting their luggage in the holding bins and beneath their seats, hoping to get another glimpse of HIM. But nothing. I shook it off. It was probably a good thing. The plane was huge and the last thing I needed was a distraction like that. Spending hours staring and imagining all kinds of dirty things that would never happen wouldn't help my plan to hook up with guys my age on this trip. Besides, I needed to sleep a few hours during this flight. The possibility of him, though, excited me more than I liked to admit.

***

I'd been down that road before, having fallen for an older guy during my sophomore year in college. Ashton had been a teaching assistant for one of my classes. By the beginning of my senior year, he'd ruined any chance I had at experiencing a decent college relationship. He'd been that typical, "too smart for his own good" doctorate student who enjoyed leading little college girls on. He'd flattered me and told me everything I had wanted to hear… and a lot I didn't. After a few months of painfully slow seduction at the back of the library, he'd confessed that his religious upbringing prevented him from moving things with me further along. By that point though, I was so enthralled with him I continued giving him clandestine blowjobs between the rows of rare books, hoping I could change his mind.

That was until I found out he had four other girls on his seduction roster. Seems Ashton enjoyed playing different roles with different people. He played the bad boy with some, the starving artist with others, and the nerdy religious guy with me. *Asshole*. He should have been a drama major.

I was a mess when it all came to an end. I was already filled with heartbreak and anger from the tragedy that took Ryan's life. He had been my high school boyfriend. Ryan had put a ring on my finger right before college started. I was too blinded by love and a shiny ring to notice that anything was ever wrong between us. Learning that he was gay after his death had broken my heart a million times over.

So yeah… I'd dated a gay guy and an older guy. That was the extent of my dating life. Both had left me with a messed-up head and feelings of inadequacy. Therapy had helped me to let go mentally. But now I needed to experience the same light, sexy, fun that my girlfriends had lived for the past few years. So an older, foreign man with a freakishly commanding presence was probably not a good option.

***

We settled into our seats and kept on chatting about the itinerary and excursions we had planned. In just a few hours, our plane would touch-down in Dublin, and #Europe2018 would begin.

CASSIDY LONDON

Chapter 2

Dublin, Ireland

Conor Murphy

The darkness came up from behind me like a fog; a billowing cloud of smoke that swirled around my head. Within seconds, I couldn't see, hear, or breathe. My heart raced as sweat poured out of me. I could feel my temperature climbing quickly, matching the speed of the revving engine that thundered in my ears. It was coming. And I knew I would feel it in my bones like I had so many times before.

Truth? You can hear it before you feel it. The crash of metal against metal, the scraping sounds in slow motion. The shattering of glass that comes moments before the shards pierce your skin. My hands covered my face and my head as I ducked down between the seats. Pain seared across my body, piercing me from end to end. Darkness covered me, but only for a moment.

My eyes opened and somehow through the dissipating fog, I saw blue skies, white clouds, and the tiniest ray of sunlight. Hope was poking through. Peace. I felt bliss take over. Suddenly, I was able to breathe deeply and feel the ecstasy as it rushed through my body, healing my wounds.

I was flying. Floating through nothing but silence.

That's when it changed. A new change. Flames of orange and red danced across my field of vision. It was getting hot, so hot, so fucking hot... I had to get out of there. I had to get to her. I knew her. I'd seen her before, but where? She was running, running away so fast, that the only part of her visible was her auburn hair that trailed behind her. I wanted to call out to her, stop her from running into the fire, but it was too late. She was gone, disappearing right through it. I couldn't save her. I heard her scream; felt her pain pierce through my heart and reverberate through my mind.

The sound of her screaming agony made me jolt awake.

My eyes opened and I was in bed alone in the darkness. A cold sweat ran across my naked body; my muscles tense with pressure and stress. Leaning back into the pillows, I ran my hands through my damp hair. Fuck. The nightmares were getting worse.

I had been plagued by recurring nightmares for years now. But something had been different this time. That fire... I never normally saw the fire. My shrink once told me it was because I was passed out by the time it started. So, what the hell had that been? Then, in just one second, I knew. It was HER. I knew I'd been a little off since that moment back in New York. As I was boarding the flight home, I had run into *her*. Well, actually, her friends had run into me. But they barely registered in my brain as anything other than an annoyance. She, however, had stood out in the crowd like a beacon of light calling to my darkness. Her rich auburn hair tempting and taunting me to put my hands in it. That lush body, those breasts that heaved up and down as she took each breath. I knew she had seen me the same way I had seen her. We were locked in a stare that only fate itself could have broken. She was so young though– too young. Young enough to still have so much to learn. And I was not a man worthy of teaching anyone the secrets of life. All these years later and I barely had my own shit together.

As usual though, my mind and my body did not agree. My cock stirred at the first sight of her, and again now as her beauty invaded my head. I imagined myself balls deep in her innocent sweet nectar. She had looked wild and fiery and I wanted nothing more than to claim her, tame her. *Own her...* Because somewhere deep inside me, I knew she already owned me.

Fuck! I adjusted my crotch as I swung my legs out of bed and marched purposefully over to the shower. A cold shower was definitely in order now. I didn't have time for this. I had to get to work. Today was a big day. We had a huge tour group coming through, and that meant I had to be on my game and the place had to be ready. Pushing all other thoughts out of my mind, I focused on the day ahead.

Thirty minutes, a shower, and a protein shake later, I was in my truck and on my way to the jump site. I started out by mentally running the checklist as I drove.

Everything needed to be in order. I couldn't leave anything to chance. Not with this kind of work, anyway. Military training had been good for that. As an ex-paratrooper who had served four tours in Afghanistan, I could easily push all thoughts out of my mind and focus in on the tiniest of details in a matter of seconds.

In my business now, just like in the army, one little mistake could cost someone their life. Sadly, I had experienced it firsthand. Back in the military, I had watched too many men get injured or lose their lives to stupid mistakes. We knew that we could die in the line of duty, and they prepared us for that, but no one should ever die because of equipment failure.

Jumping out of planes was a risky business. And whether it was in the name of freedom or just for kicks, everything had to be perfect.

The riggers would come in soon to do their final checks and pack the chutes, but I needed to go over everything first. I spent about an hour checking every chute, the reserves, and the harnesses. Going over everything meticulously made me feel calm and in control, which was exactly where I preferred to be.

After my own checks, I left everything out for the riggers to do the same. I knew I didn't have to, that's what I paid them for, but I couldn't live with myself if ever an accident happened and I hadn't checked it myself.

As owner of the "Fly the Irish Skies", I wanted all my clients– who most of the time were tourists and on their first jump- to feel calm, comfortable, and primarily safe when they jumped with us. Even if I wasn't their personal instructor.

I personally only jumped alone these days. Before the army, just like now, it was therapeutic for me. Anger had always been my go-to emotion. After the car crash that killed my family, I bounced around the foster care system. Anger consumed me and changed my personality. I was constantly being kicked out of schools and homes for fighting. Fighting was the one thing I was good at. Being big, strong, and not afraid of anyone was my identity.

I had been headed down the wrong path. School fights eventually transformed into street fights, which opened up the world of mind-numbing drugs to me. When I was high, I didn't have to remember the pain and loss to feel the anger, or the guilt, of being the only one to survive. It numbed my pain and my potential. Thankfully, a concerned teacher saw that and called me on it before it was too late. Mr. Dixon was my math teacher, and he saw in me what no one else did. He was a weekend jump-junkie and because of him, I learned that I didn't have to do drugs to get high. In fact, the best high was the adrenaline kick that came from jumping out of a moving aircraft. One weekend, he invited me to join him, and my life was changed forever. I often wonder where I would have been if he hadn't intervened in my life.

It was because of good ol' Mr. Dixon that I finished high school and joined the army. He said it would give me a healthier place to release my anger. He was right... in a way. But the army changes a person even if it saves them.

After I left the army, my demons returned, and the sweetness of mind-altering substances beckoned me back into their embrace. This time it was Eoghan who stepped in after I stumbled into his bar one too many times, high as a fucking kite. He had been the one to introduce me to his friends at the jump site, and get back in the game.

I had missed that blissful calmness of the skies. And soon the jumps gave me enough of a high that I didn't need the synthetic one anymore. I quickly got my tandem flying instructor certificate and began jumping with "sky tourists" as I called them. Weekend adrenaline junkies were amusing. People who wanted that thrill, but only once. A bucket list check-off of sorts. I didn't really understand it, but it allowed me to spend my time in the sky and that was all I cared about.

For me, skydiving was therapy. The sixty, or preferably ninety second freefall, was the only thing that calmed my mind and shut off the voices in my head. That blissful moment when you floated in a place where humans were never meant to be. If I could live in the sky permanently, I would.

Soon, my men began to gather in the main office. A morning ritual. Talking and laughing as they filled their mugs with coffee, checking their jump schedules for the day.

I always let them start off casually before I reined in their relaxed attitudes. When it came time to prep for their jumps, that's when I cracked the whip. My standards were high, and I expected the same from them. They all knew it, too. I had been through a large rotation of instructors before settling with this core group. I had hired and fired a lot of staff in those early years, constantly striving for the perfection that seemed to elude me.

They sifted through the chutes and cords. Voices were calling out to each other, checking the measurements and the buckle straps. I sorted through the paperwork for the day while the guys organized their chutes. The riggers showed up around the same time and packed. The riggers were everything in this business. Without them, we would all be taking our lives in our own hands. Most of the people who signed up to jump were tourists, and sometimes a few locals, but almost all were first-time jumpers out to check something off their bucket list.

I settled into my office to review the pre-waivers I made all our clients sign before they even showed up at the jump site. There was another waiver once they got here, but precaution was the name of game. All the cumulative paperwork did not bother me since it was what kept me and everyone aware of the actual danger of this popular activity.

Suddenly, the door to my office was flung open and in walked one of my instructors.

"Conor!" He called out. His voice was gruff with what I could only describe as frustration. "What is it, mate?" I asked.

Finn was typically my best man, but he was visibly stressed out and worried. This was not a good start to the day since our group of fifty tourists were due to arrive any minute.

"Boss, it's Dunn... he's fucking drunk again! Or at the very least, hung over."

I could feel my blood beginning to boil. My hand came across my face as I scratched my beard.

"How do you know? Are you sure?" I growled.

If there was one thing I hated, it was incompetence and no regard for the lives of others.

"Dunn!" I growled as I marched across the office and out into the open field in front of us. Dunn was there, laughing and joking with the boys. I could see the others were uncomfortable based on their body posture, and that Dunn did not understand I was about to come down hard on him. His back was to me as his arms flailed about and his voice became louder and louder. He had come to work after a night of partying. But even if he wasn't drunk, he was definitely not in the right head space to jump from an aircraft and get his passenger safely to the ground. In his state, the best-case scenario was that he'd probably vomit all over his rider, even if he got to the ground.

"Aye there, mate." I began as my hand reached out and grabbed his shoulder with enough pressure that commanded Dunn's attention. I pulled him around to face me and stared into his eyes. "'Tis the second time this month you've come in here disrespecting the job, the clients, and me, Dunn." I said firmly but in a friendly manner. I wouldn't be lenient this time around.

"Nah mate, it was a late night that's for sure, but I'm fine! Nothing a strong coffee can't cure." He looked around at the group and chuckled again. "Aye, hair of the dog- am I right?" Dunn continued searching the crowd for someone to agree with him.

Dunn stumbled a little and I gripped his shoulder harder to steady him. I knew right then I needed to put my foot down and make an impression. It was a defining moment. Either my staff would gain more respect for me and for the business in this moment, or they would lose it and everything I had worked for would take a step backwards. After everything I had built, I was not going backwards.

"Dunn. You're a good man mate, but you're not the right man for my team." I stated it bluntly and matter of fact. I wanted no misconceptions or misunderstandings.

"Conor, please man! Don't be like that!" Dunn immediately retorted.

"Y'er giving me no choice. Take your stuff and get out." I responded.

"You cannot do this!" One of the guys called out. "Who will replace him today? There's a huge group arriving soon, and we're going to be in a hole one man short!"

"I will." I answered gruffly. "It's no bother." I would not risk the lives of innocents on an arsehole who had no respect for the sport.

With that, I turned and marched back to my office. But not before I called out to Dunn yet again to go gather his things. There would be no shit-show on my watch.

Chapter 3

Dublin, Ireland

Ava Jackson

The girls and I had checked into our Dublin hotel and met the tour group for dinner on the very first night. It was awkward at first trying to get acquainted with almost fifty new faces. Luckily, Adri was the extrovert of our little group and was quick to get the conversation flowing. The trip was specifically for eighteen to twenty-five-year old's, so everyone had at least a few things in common. Many were still students but quite a few, just like us, had recently graduated too.

Adri found a cute Aussie guy to crush on by the time we were halfway through the first course. Sam and I though, took longer. We were more of the 'stand back and observe before jumping in' type of girls. Although, I wanted the full European tour experience, and there were a few potentials in our group, I still hoped we'd meet locals along the way too. Like, some foreign guy who barely spoke English just seemed like it would be much more of an authentic experience.

The next morning, we set off for a day trip to the Cliffs of Moher. What a way to start a trip. It was the most beautiful natural phenomenon that I'd ever seen. Seven hundred foot cliffs of wild limestone jutting out of the earth and overlooking the Atlantic Ocean; simply majestic.

This was definitely the start of an epic trip.

By day two though, I wanted to fucking back out of everything. It was skydiving day. And just the thought alone was making me want to feign illness. It was Adriana's idea, and in the hours leading up to the jump, it made me want to kill her for it.

It was the first of several adrenaline infused excursions on this trip, but this one was by far the worst. Jesus, if my dad knew what I was doing today, he would have fucking thrown me from the plane himself.

Naturally, I had left that part out when I gave him my itinerary. Thank goodness there was no parental waivers that needed to be signed. Being over twenty-one had many advantages.

Skydiving had never been on my bucket list, but it had been on Adri's for quite some time now. And if she was going, we all had to. That was our pact. Every time one of us chose an excursion, the rest of us had to join in, even if we weren't super thrilled about it. One for all, and all for one, or some shit like that.

The bus has been driving on a dirt road for some time now and had finally stopped next to what looked like a farm. I had noticed an old wooden sign earlier down the hill that mentioned skydiving, but where we had stopped, there seemed to be nothing more than an old dilapidated barn. We piled off the bus, and the sound of fifty people together was eerily quiet where until now had been chaotic. Panic had set in across the group.

The night before, when we had been drinking at the pub, we had been full of bravado and cocky attitudes. Egging one another on, betting on who would be the first to freak out. Things were definitely different now.

Panic wasn't even close to what I was feeling. Nausea flooded my insides, my head was spinning, and I was shrouded in a cold sweat. Leaning into Sam, I whispered to her, "So… we're really doing this, right?"

"Uh… yeah… looks like it." She muttered under her breath. "Better be fucking worth it." She continued casually, rolling her eyes.

I laughed at her attempt to make this okay. We were about to jump out of a moving aircraft at fourteen thousand feet. There was nothing casual about any of it.

The guides ushered us into a miniature version of the main barn-type shelter. It was empty, save for some hay on the ground and a flat screen TV mounted on the wall. Chickens were running by, and the clearing surrounding the barn was a somber looking dense forest. It was extremely quiet out here, so far from civilization. No sounds from traffic, not even birds were flying about.

For the price we had paid, this place did not look as professional as the brochures had made it out to be. I could only hope they spent their money on training the instructors more than on the décor.

A guy came over and explained that we were to watch a video on skydiving, then sign the paperwork before the training began.

"When do we suit up mate?" Called out one of the Aussies from our group.

"Only once you know what the hell you've gotten yourself into!" Was the response, as the instructor tipped his imaginary hat and walked away and back into the office. *Shit.* A collective nervous chuckle reverberated through the crowd as the video began. We watched in silence as it started out with images of professional skydivers in formations and competitions. Gasps and laughs of sounds of "That'd better not be what we're doing today" was audible across the group.

Finally, tandem jumps began showing up on the video. We watched instructors jumping out of planes strapped to tourists just like us. A lot of the same instructors we'd seen in and around the site were also on the video. It was comforting that the people we were watching in the video were also standing a few feet away from us sipping their coffee. I breathed a sigh of relief as I repeated to myself: *They've all jumped hundreds of times and lived to do it again.* Watching them in the flesh was a lot more interesting than watching the video. They were calm and relaxed, and yet, slightly jittery and fidgety every few minutes as they looked up to the sky. Some of them had a look that could only be described as anxious or in need of a hit.

One of the guys must have realized that I was watching him shift his weight from foot to foot, revealing what seemed to be a nervous demeanor.

"No worries lass, just a little jittery. We haven't been up in a few days." He began.

"What do you mean?" I asked.

"Ceiling's been too low the last few days. So we haven't jumped. But finally, clear skies and sunshine today!" He continued, smiling and pointing up to the sky.

Just then, someone called out from the office that the ceiling was at nine thousand feet, which meant we'd be jumping in under an hour. I sucked air in and then slowly exhaled, trying to calm myself. *C'mon Ava. You can do this.*

"Oh, my God!" Screeched Adri. "I can't believe we're going up there! I've waited forever for this!" Sam and I looked at each other nervously and smiled. "Maybe there's still time to back out?" Sam mouthed.

The instructors moved our group over to a tented area with picnic tables. They told us to wait there until the owner of the skydiving school arrived, as he would be the one giving the lesson.

I silently wondered how much we needed to know, and if I would even remember it all as I was freefalling out of a plane at two thousand feet per second. Hopefully, the tandem instructor would do all the work and I would just be along for the ride.

Suddenly, the instructor that had directed us to this space called out, "Can I have your attention everyone?" We all looked up nervously. "I'd like to introduce you to the owner of the "Fly the Irish Skies". This is Conor Murphy. Mr. Murphy has been jumping for about twenty years now…?" He looked over to his boss for confirmation. Getting the head nod he wanted, he continued. "He's an ex-military paratrooper who fell in love with the sky so much he didn't want to leave it, even once his final tour ended." Laughter broke out in the group as their semi-circle broke apart and a huge monster of a man stepped forward. I felt the tightness in my chest even before I heard myself gasp. His emerald green eyes scanned the crowd and seemed to zero in on me within seconds. I was so fucked. The pull of a familiar yet otherworldly vortex was calling my name.

"Holy shit!" Whispered Sam under her breath.

"I don't fucking believe it." Adri chimed in.

I couldn't say a word. It was too crazy. What an insane coincidence that the man from JFK airport was now standing in front of us in Dublin, about to explain what we were to expect on our virgin skydiving experience.

Heat engulfed my senses. I gasped for air. Reaching out to steady myself on Adriana was my only option for trying to contain myself.

Would he recognize us? Me? Was I the only one feeling this weird sensation? Why did I feel like he was looking right at me?

It quickly became a fight to hold myself together. My cheeks felt flushed and I could feel the uncomfortable red splotches forming across my chest. Trying to hide it, I crossed my arms and sat casually in my hip, using my long hair to hide my face as my body betrayed me.

He was physically massive. Biceps and pectorals that went on for days. Shaggy, dirty-blond hair that was pushed back, and a beard that emphasized his strong jawline. Tattoos ran up the side of his forearms and down on to the backs of his hands. He was already suited up in a jumpsuit, which made me wonder if he dressed like that because he was the owner, or because he had plans to jump today.

Clearing his throat, Conor Murphy addressed the crowd. That raspy Irish accent was so sexy, I felt myself falling under his spell and becoming more and more mesmerized by the second. Watching him explain the ropes and ties, buckles and harness, and what they did was like watching an uncomfortable yet addicting beautiful ballet. He knew what he was talking about, and it was easy to tell how comfortable he was with the equipment. He explained how all we had to do was be in the right emotional state to enjoy ourselves and hold our body position. There were two positions we needed to remember, but if we forgot, then our instructor would remind us.

As he talked, my mind was on overdrive trying to come up with a question to ask or a reason to talk to him. Zoning back in, I heard him discuss the moment that had me most terrified. The free-fall.

"The free-fall is the sixty to ninety second fall from the plane, depending on the height you have jumped from, before your parachute deploys. The only thing you need to remember during the free-fall is to keep your arms crossed and hold the harness until you feel your instructor tap you on the shoulder. When he gives you the signal, release your arms into the open position and bend your knees to place your feet up behind him." Conor continued. "Now folks, this is the part that most likely terrifies you the most, am I right?" he asked, rolling those r's in that accent, which completely distracted me. The crowd erupted in agreement. Conor smiled. *Fuck that was a killer smile.* "You shall soon see that what scares you the most is actually the moment

40

you'll come to remember most fondly, long after this bucket list excursion is done."

Although I heard his words, it was his eyes that held me captive. They shone with a passion so strong and so clear. He loved what he did, that was obvious, but it seemed to be even more than that. He spoke wistfully about the skies and how we would soon see that the feeling of flying was incomparable to anything else.

"It's like being in another world. A blissfully silent place that just shuts off your brain and lets you feel." When he finished, everyone was silent. Somehow, his descriptions had made this moment seem less stressful. I felt an eagerness to understand his words even better.

"Anyhow, it's time to suit up. My boys haven't been up there in two days and they're feeling the pain, right lads?" He asked the instructors. They hollered a happy response. "A few days without a jump is like an addict without a fix." He finished, still staring right at me.

I tried to absorb his words, which was a little easier whenever he averted his gaze to another part of the crowd. But when his line of focus drifted back in my direction, there was nothing I could think of other than his hands on my body. I could feel myself getting flustered at my own thoughts and silently wondered what my friends would say. He was older than I first noticed back in New York. Definitely closer to forty than thirty. But it didn't matter, not to me anyway. He was the hottest man here, and he kept starting at ME.

Lost in thought, I didn't notice when Adam, another American from our group, had come and stood next to me. In fact, it barely registered when he casually put his arm around me and whispered in my ear. "Wonder when the last time Sargent up there jumped. He's so damn cocky and insistent that we understand all this shit. I want to fucking jump already!" Nodding politely, I sidestepped a little. He moved with me, his arm sliding down to my waist. "Besides…" he continued, "the instructor takes care of everything in a tandem jump, we're just along for the ride."

Adam touching me was uncomfortable. I squirmed again to remove his arm. Like a dead weight on my body, it felt heavy and just plain wrong. He didn't seem to notice, though. He kept on chatting away as I pretended to listen, still locked into that magnetic green gaze as I looked past Adam. It had changed though. His look had become even more intense, almost to the point of showing irritation. He stared at Adam, fury flooding his eyes.

"Don't make light of this, it is serious. We're taking our lives in our hands, you know." I whispered to Adam. Adam just chuckled as he pulled me in closer.

"Hey mate!" The voice sent shivers up my spine. I closed my eyes, preparing myself for a possible confrontation.

Adri, who was standing in front of me, turned her head to look at me and whispered under her breath, "Ava! He's been staring at you this whole time!"

I attempted to shake off Adam's arm and feeling flustered, I quickly smoothed over my clothing.

"You! Mate-", Rumbled the voice again.

I looked up. He was standing right in front of Adam now, towering above him. Adam was a tall guy, maybe five-foot eleven, but Conor Murphy was like a giant next to him.

"What I'm explaining here today can save y'er life. But if you think y'er too good for that and you know better, then so be it. Get out and you can take y'er jump elsewhere." Conor's accent had come out full force, which could only mean he was truly irritated.

Heat seemed to emanate off his body as his chest heaved with the weight of his words. Passionate and wild, he looked like he was about to pick up Adam by the scruff of his neck and throw him across the field.

He was standing so close I could smell him. It wasn't a cologne or aftershave or anything fake like that, just the clean smell of a rugged man straight out of the shower. I inhaled deeply, and felt myself shudder as his scent went spiraling down into my body. I rolled my eyes and flicked my hair in an effort to shake off my reaction to him. For the briefest of moments, his bare arm, hard, toned, and warm, brushed mine and the hairs on my skin rose. My entire body was on high alert.

Did he notice?

His eyes flickered, but just for a split second before he made an abrupt turn and walked off.

Adam was visibly shaken, but it was his pride that was broken more than anything. "Fuck this shit!" He called out. "If you think I will trust anyone to protect my life when you have zero respect for me as a customer, then you've got another thing coming big guy!" His words spewed out like vomit across the crowd.

Conor just waved him away before encouraging the crowd to follow him into the field to the landing site. "C'mon this way everyone. I want you to see where you'll be landing." I felt shaky, but I grabbed onto Sam's arm as we looked at each other knowingly, understanding how intense and unexpected his reaction had been. We all marched together across a muddy field and into a bigger clearing than the one we were in before.

Chapter 4

Dublin, Ireland

Conor Murphy

It was HER. It couldn't have been anyone else. As much as the thought of this happening was almost too much for my brain to comprehend, I knew it was her. That hair... fiery auburn red, and that skin, so pale but for the tiniest of freckles spattered across her nose. But it was the flush of blood rising to the surface of her skin as she saw me that nearly took me down. I watched as the realization of who I was instantly crossed her face. Her beautiful eyes drank in the comprehension, her pupils dilating in surprise and appreciation.

As I explained the equipment to the group, I struggled to keep my mind focused and my body in check. It was like being at war again. Everything in my being was telling me to run, but I knew it was not an option. Fortunately, I was familiar with these contradictory feelings. My whole life had been a constant battle between animalistic instinct and intellectual knowledge.

I continued to explain how to put on the jumpsuit and the base harness. Some visitors seemed taken aback, thinking they had to secure the harness themselves. I assured them that their instructor would tighten and secure all the buckles and ropes, but that it was still in their best interest to know how things worked.

We went over body positioning and silent instructions as that would be the only way to communicate once in the air.

"Truly, the only things you need to remember," I reminded the group, "is that when your instructor taps you on the right shoulder, you release your arms from the jump position and open them." I demonstrated as I spoke, extending my arms up to the sky, keeping my elbows bent and my hands straight, palms facing forward.

"Now the legs…" I paused and scanned the group, trying to distract myself from staring only at her. *What was her name?* A sea of petrified faces stared back at me. I looked for the cocky ones, as experience told me that there was always one or two. I scanned the lines from one end to the other and finally back to where I couldn't stay away from. She stared at me, in full comprehension now, but with something more. *Desire.* Her full pouty lips beckoned to be sucked. She sat on her hip which only accentuated her full round ass. Hands on her hips, she rolled her eyes as my gaze skimmed over her as if to taunt me. *Fuck!* Her body language, intentional or not, only made my damn cock stir even more beneath the tightness of my jeans under my suit.

Just like the color of her hair suggested, she was a hot little firecracker. With that tight little body and sassy look on her face, it only made me want to break her even more. My thoughts both excited and disturbed me. She was so young. Too young. At least twenty, but probably not much more. No wonder she looked at me with disgust. Even though I wasn't forty yet, I was probably nothing more than an old man to her.

An old guy with a lifetime of demons he still hadn't tamed. Some catch I was. No wonder relationships were off-limits for me. I had nothing to offer. At least not to someone like her, anyway. I sighed. Still though, the thought of taking her over my knee and spanking some sense into that little one was so tempting. Then, images of massaging her bare creamy white ass over my knees flashed in my mind, and I lost my trail of thought several times.

She was too distracting. I needed to stay on course and give this group the right training. I looked for someone or something else to grab my attention. It didn't take long before I realized that the cocky bastard I'd been looking for was actually standing right next to the beautiful girl. I watched as he slid up to her like a snake, putting his hands on her luscious body as his motivation. He whispered in her ear and pulled her in close despite her obvious disgust with him. I would have no choice but to put him in his place. She was much too good for an idiot like that. Maybe I had been at this too long, or it was truly my age, but reading men's behavior with trying to bag a woman was somewhat of a specialty of mine. And for some reason, I felt possessive of this girl, and I was not going to let some stupid bloke half my age seduce her on my land no less.

Finally, I finished up the lesson and instructed everyone to head over to the office for the weigh-in. Weigh-ins were a crucial part of teaming up the right instructor with the right client. There was only a certain amount of weight that the chute could hold, so matching up the right people was basically a lifesaving task to ensure that no one got injured or worse.

The ladies always hated this part. They would try to take off as much as possible to weigh less. That's why I insisted on weighing them after they had their jumpsuits on.

After they were all dressed, we weighed them one by one and assigned an instructor to each one. From here on, my guys took over, making the clients feel comfortable, and the all-important tying them into their harness.

I focused on getting everyone organized when Pat leaned over and whispered in my ear. "Conor, we all fucking hate you right now, man." Looking up in surprise, I raised one eyebrow. "Why?" I growled out, annoyed at his words and for being disturbed.

"Don't tell me you haven't figured it out yet?" He chuckled in surprise. "It's obvious who you get to jump with." He muttered as he walked away to his client.

Shit. I had forgotten that I was jumping. With everything that had gone down already, and the distraction of *her*, it had made me forget the altercation and ultimate firing of Dunn this morning.

"Next!" I called out without looking up. I kept my focus down on the ground near the scale. A small pair of white Adidas runners stepped onto the scale. Tiny delicate ankles rose from above them, one of them decorated with a string of multi-colored beads. My cock stirred again. *When the fuck had the sight of runners ever turned me on?* Ever so slowly, I let my gaze travel upwards. I could still see her shapely legs through the jumpsuit. Full, bouncy hair that rested on her shoulders and smelled like flowers. I paused watching as her perky breasts lifted and lowered with each breath. I wanted to see them bursting from that zipper, which held them secured nice and tight. Even through the jumpsuit, I could see how heavy they would rest in the palms of my hands. She had left the collar of the suit open, and a delicate milky white collarbone peaked out. I imagined what her soft skin would feel like under my lips. Finally, when I couldn't hide it any longer, I looked her right in the eyes. Smoldering beacons of caramel stared back at me. Each iris was lightly flecked with spots that mimicked the freckles across her nose.

Her face crumpled up into a question of sorts, somewhat worried, somewhat wanting. "What does it say?" she asked, her lovely voice throatier than I had imagined. Visions of grabbing hold of her hair and pulling her into my mouth flooded my mind, the silky, soft skin on her neck beneath the harshness of my beard, all while ripping that zipper down as fast as I could.

Maintain focus, Conor.

"It says you're jumping with me." I answered gruffly as I turned and walked away.

Chapter 5

Dublin, Ireland

Ava Jackson

I stood there, frozen with shock. *He was going to be* **MY** *instructor?* By the look on his face, he would probably throw me out of the plane on my own. He did not in any way look as if he would be helpful in calming my already shot nerves. Fuck… he was hot, though. I felt my entire body fidget nervously in his presence. Heat had built up around me like a sauna. An aching from deep within my core came out of nowhere and pounded my body from the inside out. Even my hair seemed to stand up to attention as I began to sweat. He had an effect on me unlike anything I'd experienced before. This was not good… but it sure felt good.

I glanced sideways over to my girls but they didn't notice me. They were too busy chatting away with their instructors and getting harnessed up. Adriana was positively glowing with excitement. Sam looked like she wanted to puke but was trying hard to smile through it. Everyone else from our group was already paired off and I seemed to be the only one left. I stood there a minute, chewing my lip and trying to decide what options I had left. It's not that I minded being strapped to the Irish "Adonis", just more like I was afraid of how I felt being so close to him. Body heat would be involved here. He would be straddling me from behind; there would be physical contact without a doubt. And I was terrified. I had signed up to jump fourteen thousand feet from a moving aircraft. *What the hell was I thinking?*

"MISS!" Growled that deep, raspy, oh-so-sexy voice. I whipped around and stared. His hand held high in the air, he beckoned me towards him. "Over here!" He shouted at me. *Why was that so exciting?* Being ordered. It sort of made me feel naughty even if I had not done anything wrong.

"Hey! I called out as I jogged over to where he stood, holding a mass of buckles, harnesses, and ropes. "Something to say?" he asked as I came to a full stop in front of him. I looked up into those emerald eyes. "We met back at the airport in New York, remember?"

"No, I don't." he answered. "Now step in here..." he continued, motioning for me to step through an opening in the harness. "And listen to everything I say. You must listen and do exactly as I say so that you enjoy this jump safely, understood lass?"

Okay... clearly, he was all business and either didn't remember or didn't want to socialize. At least thinking about him took my mind off the jump for a few brief moments. I nodded and made sure my eyes confirmed I understood him.

This wasn't going down the way I wanted it to, but I was going to have to make the best of it… and so was he. Flashing him with my megawatt smile, I twirled a strand of hair around my fingers. "It's Conor, right?" I chewed on my bottom lip, hoping to soften him up a little.

He paused. His cold stare bore through me like a knife, making me shiver uncomfortably in the summer heat. He took a step forward, momentarily blocking out the sun. I was left feeling dwarfed by his oversized and almost arrogant presence.

"Yeah, Conor's the name." He finally answered.

"My apologies. It's been a rough morning here. But I promise you'll enjoy every minute of this jump." He continued, professionalism now back in full swing. "First time?" he asked, avoiding eye contact. I giggled. Maybe a little harmless flirting would soften him up and make this more enjoyable…

"Yeah… can you tell how nervous I am?" I continued, feeling slightly light headed all of a sudden. The corners of his eyes creased as he smiled in acknowledgment.

"Actually, this was my girlfriend Adriana's idea, but…" I proceeded to tell Conor all about our trip and the bets we had made with each other. I found myself getting lost in my story as I babbled on nervously, barely noticing that he didn't seem to be paying any attention.

He said nothing as he motioned for me to step into what looked like an adult size baby carrier. The straps went around each thigh and up over each shoulder with another around my waist. I followed his lead. I took advantage while I slipped into the harness to look at his ring finger. It was empty; he had no rings on either hand.

"ENOUGH!" He suddenly yelled in my face, his palm face up in front of me. "Stop talking! You need to listen."

Damn, he was so bossy! Somehow that made him sexier though... *shit.* Why hadn't I been thinking like this about the guys on the trip? Those were the ones I needed to be getting nervous around. Not some way-too-old-for-me skydiving instructor that I'd never see again. *He was local though... I did say I wanted authentic local experiences...* The battlefield in my mind continued.

"I need to tighten the straps, alright?" He spoke more softly now, almost gentle. "It may be uncomfortable now, but that's what we need in the air, okay? After the freefall, I'll loosen them if they are hurting you." His hands ran across the harness that rested on my body. Even through the straps and the jumpsuit, his touch felt like fire through the layers.

"Uh... okay?" I responded, squinting into the sunlight to see him, unsure as to what that even meant.

Conor then bent down on one knee. His face was now almost in line with mine and it gave me the opportunity to really study it. I found myself wanting to reach out and touch those cheekbones, that beard, his hair. Closer up, his eyes were even more hypnotizing. The "emerald isle" herself could have been modeled after those eyes. This is what locals nicknamed Ireland. His stare was direct, with a hint of fire behind it that only made me want to see more of him.

His hands wrapped around the straps that loosely circled each of my thighs. They were huge and seemed as if they could easily break me. As he grabbed the buckle, his eyes looked up into mine. "I'm going to tighten the right side now, miss." *Oh…my…God.* The intimacy of this moment was clearly affecting me. And the way he spoke was wetting my panties. His confidence, and commands, layered with obvious permission to have his hands all over me, well, I was so fucked…

Conor then pulled so hard that the straps shot up my thigh, landing right under my ass. I could feel them digging into the sensitive skin inside my thigh, tugging slightly around my privates. The shock made me accidentally exhale and grab his shoulder to steady myself. *And… that sounded like a moan. Great going Ava.* I wanted to bury my face in my hands.

"Too tight?" He questioned, amusement registering on his face. His eyes glinted with a little naughtiness to them.

"Not at all." I responded indifferently. There was no way I was admitting to that.

"All right, the other one then." He proceeded to pull the left side just as hard as the right until I felt like my ass plumping out behind me was possibly making it larger than any of the Kardashian's fake asses. My jumpsuit now felt tighter than ever and my thong was riding up my ass in the worst way... I could see Conor eyeing my body and taking note of what felt like was a wedgie and a camel toe all at the same time. Uncomfortable– yes. On display– fuck yes!

His eyes twinkled in amusement. Clearly my being uncomfortable was amusing to him. *Very fucking professional.*

"Now the top." He pulled the straps so hard that both my shoulders were yanked back instantly, giving me perfect posture. "The next one goes right here... excuse me... miss." He breathed as he attached the harness across my chest, skimming the underside of my breasts. "Ava... call me Ava." I whispered as the heat flushed across my cheeks. He had both hands over my ribcage and just below my breasts. They were so large, they were able to span my entire torso. His every touch was making it harder to breathe.

"As you wish, Ava. Ready?" He questioned. I nodded

and looked to the side. *Why was this fucking harness turning me on so much?*

Conor pulled the cord and the chest straps tightened. Now my breasts were sticking out, inches away from his mouth. I felt like a trapped bird ensnared in a fishing net. It was both exhilarating and comforting, evoking the strangest sensation of being nervous and yet calm at the same time. The tightness of the harness seemingly contained my terror at a manageable level.

He stared at me, scanning my body and making me self-conscious in a way I hadn't felt before. Those emerald pools seemed to want to eat me up. I wasn't sure how to interpret his reaction to me. "Too tight?" he asked. I nodded to confirm. "But it doesn't hurt." I added.

He smiled. "Good. You may just be tougher than you look, Ava." He finished before winking and walking away.

CASSIDY LONDON

Chapter 6

Dublin, Ireland

Conor Murphy

Tying her up in that harness had made my cock throb for her so badly. *What was wrong with me, lusting after such a young thing?* That tight little body straining against the buckles and straps made me want to see her naked and restrained in my bed. I could just imagine the tight ropes across her soft white skin and the red marks they would leave behind. I wanted to look into her eyes as she fought the urge to fight back and the eventual submission and softness that would overtake her body. I imagined pleasuring her soft pink folds between her legs with my tongue. Her smell was already intoxicating to me, I could only imagine what she would taste like, especially restrained in a way that would keep her open and wet for me. A flash of us freefalling naked except for the harnesses came into my mind.

Fuck! I needed to concentrate. I turned away to discreetly adjust my crotch and attempt to regain control. Control was typically very easy for me. *Why was this different? She was different.*

She didn't look at me like the others did. Typically, I could read women well. Ava was attracted and intrigued by me, yes, but what was different was that she didn't seem to assume she could have me. I was used to it at the jump site, in bars; hell, sometimes even walking down the street. Women, and in particular tourists, tended to throw themselves my way.

Ava didn't.

She seemed almost shy and unaware of her beauty. Uncertainty seemed to hold her back. Or maybe I was reading her wrong and she wasn't interested? After all, I was probably an old man to her. Or maybe she was taken? Nah. That couldn't be it, she was on a European vacation with girlfriends. No boyfriend in his right mind would have allowed her to take a trip like that without him. She was too damn beautiful. In any case, as much as I wanted her, she wasn't mine for the taking.

I had known she was too young when I first saw her, but after glancing at her waiver, I now knew she was twenty-two. Two years older than I had first assumed, but still. A baby in comparison with my thirty-eight years. Besides, girls like her didn't go out looking for fucked up PTSD ridden war vets. This was the kind of girl who needed a solid guy by her side. I could barely take care of myself on a daily basis. But what I could do was ensure she had a great jump. Her and everyone else who was here, putting their lives in my hands.

I broke up the large group into smaller groups of four pairs. Ava and I would jump last after her two friends and their instructors. I was always the last man out of the plane and today was no exception.

"Hey Conor!" That sweet voice called my name. It tinkled like a chime in the wind. That sound would have been much sweeter had it been screaming my name as she came... *FUCK!*

Shaking my head to toss out the thoughts that clouded my mind, I looked in her direction. "Can we jump first?" She asked, her voice shaking a little. "I'm so nervous, I think I'm going to bail otherwise!"

I could hear the panic creeping up through each word. She was fighting for control but the fear on her face gave away her emotions. Those soft liquid caramel eyes were filled with worry.

"Sorry Ava. But I have to go last. 'Tis my responsibility to ensure that everything goes well across the board before I jump."

"What about another instructor?" She continued, her words spilling out even faster this time. "I–I can't do this... I don't even want to do this."

"Don't move!" I told her. I ran across the field and into the office. Quickly checking the controls, I radioed ahead to the pilot to make sure everything was ready for the first jump, then put one of my men on watch as the first group boarded.

I was about to break all my rules for this girl.

Even from a number of feet away I could see that she was shaking like a leaf. Her friends had gathered in an attempt to comfort her, but she was clearly in the throes of a panic attack.

Her friend Adriana could be heard saying "Ava honey, it will be fun! You'll love it, I promise!" It seemed more like Adriana wanted this for herself, and didn't want Ava to ruin it for her.

I stayed close but stood back surveying the situation. Samantha was more sympathetic. With her arms around Ava, she gently caressed her face, pushing her hair back and rubbing her back saying "Shhh…" as if to calm a baby. Sweet, but ineffective.

I knew what she needed.

"Sean! Mike!" I called out to my guys. "Take these girls on the next jump, I'll be waiting here until everyone has returned."

Time to break rule number one. "I'll be going up alone with Ava."

"Uh… really boss?" Sean looked at me quizzically. They both knew that wasting valuable gas on one jumper was never an option. I hated being wasteful, but for some reason, I just wanted her all to myself.

"'Yeah, it's fine. Now go!" I barked back, motioning them towards the plane as I threw my arm around Ava and walked her over to a nearby bench.

"You going to be okay, hon?" Samantha called out, looking over her shoulder.

Ava just managed a weak smile as she nodded and waved to her friends. She was still shaking and her eyes began to fill with tears as she looked up at me. I needed to shake her out of this negative state. Maybe a little shock would do it.

Rule number two- broken.

I waited until the last group was out of sight before grabbing the harness that rested on her shoulders. I lifted up her small frame and threw her over my shoulder with ease. Her tight little ass was now protruding out of my left shoulder right near my ear. She squealed as I grabbed at her thighs and ass to steady her, but she made no attempt to move and scream. "Stay still, Ava." I cautioned.

Keeping one hand on the back of her knees and the other over the small of her back above her ass, I jogged part of the way back to the office. Fear and panic had overtaken her, but as soon I took her by surprise and roughed her up a little, she had relaxed beneath my touch. For the second time this morning.

I slammed the door to the office shut behind me with my foot. I set her back down on her feet. She stumbled for a second before crossing her arms, cocking her head, and sitting in her hip. Anger flashed across her face as she prepared to give me shit. *God help me, she was even cuter when she was pissed.*

"What the hell was that?" She demanded.

"Can't let panic take over you, lass." I answered confidently. "It's actually a proven fact that the best way to stop fear is to have it jolted out of you."

She just stared.

What the fuck was I saying? She must think I'm crazy now. She was not going to fall for my bullshit.

Minutes passed and I watched her face soften and her breathing hitch. I stepped closer, invading her personal space and staring down into her soft brown eyes. I imagined unzipping that jumpsuit slowly, watching her breasts pop out just for me, her body naked underneath it, and fucking her luscious body right over the goddamn front desk. I pictured her screaming my name, sweat beneath her breasts squeaking on the finish while I rammed her hard and paperwork went flying off the desk, taking the phones with it.

Shit. Any more thoughts like this and I would be taking her to bed before this day was over. I shut off the voices in my head and pressed forward. "You want to do this? Do you want to jump? Answer honestly, Ava."

"Yes, I do. Well, at first I didn't, but I also don't want to miss out on the experience. I'm just so scared."

"Okay, good. Then let's do this my way okay? Tandem jumps are very safe. The equipment is top notch and there's even a reserve chute." She nodded slowly. I breathed a sigh of relief. "I've jumped out of thousands of planes. Do you trust me?" Ava nodded yes.

"Perfect. Now, I also suggest a safe word." I couldn't help myself, I was purposely trying to ruffle her up for my own enjoyment.

"A what now?" She pulled a face, half surprised, half intrigued.

"You know, a safe word. It's just in case we get up there and you really do change your mind." Ava nodded slowly as if considering the idea. "Typically, people start saying they've changed their mind as we approach the drop off point. However, when given the choice to say a completely unrelated word that would turn the plane around, they do think twice."

"So… it's like a fifty-shades kind of thing?" Her mocking tone sparked unexpected anger in me.

"NO!" I growled. "Not like that at all. Besides, that was…" I sucked in air so hard my chest hurt.

"That was not… what?" She was turning my little game

on me.

"Not the same thing at all." Was all I could manage

"Okay, but relax. Don't get so pissed about it." She smiled, her panic completely gone now. "How about we go with Pineapple?"

"Fine. Pineapple." I repeated back to her.

Chapter 7

Dublin, Ireland

Ava Jackson

This was fucked up. My emotions were all over the place. My body was acting like it had a mind of its own. And I had just suggested to this grown man that shouting *Pineapple* as a safe word if I was too terrified to jump, was a good idea.

Most of the entire tour group had already jumped. Adri and Sam were next. Conor had made me stay inside the office during everyone's jumps as he watched from the monitors. He had agreed to let me see my friends though.

It was weird. The more time I spent one-on-one with him, the more it felt like I had known him for a long time. I found myself listening and following his directions. I trusted him. His gruff voice, instead of startling me like it did at the beginning, was comforting. He was just a little rough around the edges, but it just meant he was serious and professional. His military background must have had a lot to do with it.

However, something was changing and it was changing fast. And the feeling was becoming even more intoxicating than the mounting sexual tension between us.

We walked out into the field to watch the girls land. Conor explained that when you're jumping from fourteen thousand feet, we would only see them as they descended in the parachute slowly. I strained my eyes to look up into the sky waiting for them to come into focus. Suddenly, a small floating ant like creature came out of nowhere.

"Over there!" I cried, wildly jumping up and down. "Adri! Sam! Oh my God! You did it!" I called out to them, waving like a mad person.

I felt him staring at me. As I turned my head, I saw his eyes drinking me in and a smile forming on his lips. "They can't see you yet, you know that, right?" He chuckled.

"Uh… of course, right." I mumbled and felt myself flushing. *Totally thought they could.*

We watched as they floated down softly to earth. As soon as they hit the ground, I couldn't help myself and ran over closer to their landing spot.

"How was it?" I called out. "Fucking amazing Ava!" Adriana called back to me, still catching her breath.

"Get your ass up there and DO IT!" Sam screeched.

Just then, Conor's hand laid heavily on my shoulder. "You ready?" He asked, his voice steady but strong.

"Yes…. yes, I am." His calming masculine presence gave me confidence.

My friends were clearly thrilled with the experience and a part of me wished I had gone up with them. That thought only crossed my mind for a split second, though. As soon as Conor pulled at my hand to follow him towards the plane, bile came up into my throat. Nausea began to overwhelm me and adrenaline shot through my veins.

"No– no, Conor I don't know…" I faltered as he gathered up the last remaining items and ushered me towards the jump plane.

"Pineapple already?" He joked, actually making me laugh. "Come on Ava… you just said you wanted to do this. Let's at least get into the plane before you decide." He suggested. "Worst case, we go up, look around, and come back down."

"Okay fine, no. I'm good. Let's do this." I answered, pushing back the nerves into that dark hole from which they came. It was time to be a big girl.

I knew I would hate myself tomorrow if I didn't at least try. Especially after Sam had done it. She had been just as scared as I was. If she did it and seemed to love it, then so would I. I couldn't be a chicken-shit on day one of this trip.

Conor and I approached the plane, if you could even

call it that. It was smaller than a Cessna and looked older than I was. For all his talk about safety, he could have offered a better-looking plane. He ushered me in front of him, placing his hand on my head as we bent down to climb inside.

It was basically a metal box. A tin can. Two simple benches and more harnesses and ropes than I'd ever seen strewn across the floor of a cabin. Buckles hanging from the panels swaying slightly. Tiny windows and a clear view of the pilot, who was practically in the same cabin with us. This is how small this plane was.

The pilot could only be described as a stereotypical stoner. Just like the ones from my college, he was shirtless. He wore a sarong and a million bracelets up his tattooed arms. His long, shaggy, dirty hair was covered by his outback hat. A pair of goggles sitting atop of a scarf that was wrapped around his neck completed his crazy look. He was sipping a coffee (at least I hoped it was coffee), and as I looked down, I noticed he was wearing rubber boots. He looked better suited to attend Burning Man in the Nevada desert instead of flying a plane.

"MATE!" Called the pilot as he turned his head to fist pump Conor and wink at me. Conor nodded and smirked as he sat down and motioned for me to do the same.

I was shaking so hard I could barely move. Conor leaned forward and yelled in my ear to sit down. There was no whispering once the engine was on. The loud roar was unmistakable. We were minutes away from leaving solid ground.

Still, I didn't move.

He reached over and cupped his hands around my ear. "What's your word Ava? Do you remember your safe word?" I nodded. "Do you need to use it?" He was dangling it in front of me, testing me. I didn't want to use it, not yet anyway. I shook my head saying no. He smiled and wrapped his arms around my waist, pulling me down onto his lap on the bench. Our bodies connected, sending sparks of desire through me. Wrapped in his arms, it hit me hard how much his touch excited me. I could feel the heat of his thighs and his entire body through our jumpsuits, despite the situation.

And also, I became aware that we were not yet tied together.

"Wait! Wait!" I called out as he slid me off his lap and pushed me down to sit, spreading my legs over each side of the bench. "We're not tied together yet!" I cried out, wildly grabbing at the straps and buckles.

"I know what I'm doing, Ava! Stop moving!" He barked as he clipped my harness to a buckle on the wall. "You have to be attached to the plane until five thousand feet. Then I will tie you to my body."

"Oh, okay… sorry." I mumbled sheepishly.

"Trust, Ava… this is all about trust. Work through the fear and trust that there is something better on the other side."

I nodded. I wanted that, I really did.

Conor then signaled to the pilot and within seconds, someone from outside shut the door and the plane began to slowly move towards the runway. It was loud and shaky and felt like a tin can rattling onward. I wasn't even sure the plane would be able to take off from the ground. We picked up speed and as we did, Conor motioned for me to look out the window. I saw all his team, my tour group, and most importantly, my girls all cheering for us outside. They were waving and jumping up and down like crazy. I couldn't hear them but seeing them all was enough to make me feel their love.

Conor kept his hands wrapped around my shoulders, occasionally rubbing my arms up and down. The motion was comforting and I felt myself begin to relax as I leaned back into him. I turned my head to look at him as I felt the plane lift itself from the ground. Surprised to see he had a helmet on, I motioned to him asking where mine was and he shook his head. Putting his hand on my forehead, he reminded me that my head needed to rest on his shoulder. Remembering the information from the class he had given, I nodded and looked back outside to wave to my friends who were quickly becoming tiny ants on the ground.

Just a few minutes of looking outside at the green quilted countryside, I was lost in momentary thought at how beautiful it all was. Ireland looked untouched from up here. I could never forget this. Conor tapped me on my shoulder to show me that it was time to change the harness. He unclipped mine from the panel and began attaching it to his. And just like that, I snapped back to reality and the present.

He grabbed my harness and pulled me into his body. It was like slamming into a hard sheet of rock. I softened on impact and felt myself mold into his chest. We were so close. It was intimate invading each other's personal space like this. If I was his girlfriend, I would not be happy knowing this is how my man spent his days; touching and being attached to strangers this intimately all day. Even more awkward was feeling the hard bulge beneath his jumpsuit digging into my ass. It was absolutely a hard-on. *Was this erotic to him?* He pulled again and began tightening all the buckles and straps. It hurt to be tied that tightly, but it also made me feel safer. Every time he asked if I was okay, I motioned to him to pull tighter and I could swear his eyes sparkled. My mind felt dazed and consumed by his scent and his hands all over my body. He was most definitely reassuring me over and over by stroking his warm palms over my arms between adjustments. He probably felt it was the only way to keep me calm.

He continued checking to see if I was okay as he continued to tighten and lock everything in. His constant concern made me feel safer. He even tested out my safe word by whispering it in my ear. His hot breath tickled my ear despite the situation we were in. I shook my head for "no". For now, anyway...

I looked outside again; we were going higher and higher. As if reading my mind, he showed me the altimeter so I would know our height. Eight thousand feet. I knew some people jumped from here, but he had told me that it was too low and didn't give the same experience. If I was going to do it, I was going to do it right.

Finally, he motioned that we were two minutes away from jumping.

That was when the adrenaline began to turn into excitement. It was surprising and magical and I never saw it coming. I had expected to be crying and screaming my safe word, but instead, my mind had begun to cross over into a space that was both beautifully calm and freeing.

The door to the plane opened and for a split second, I

was aware that I had never been inside a plane with the door open before. And we weren't being sucked out like in the movies, either. The sensation was so wrong yet so right. *Surreal.*

Conor pushed me forward and we began to move closer to the open door. Next thing I knew, we were sitting on the edge and the wind was rushing by. I looked up at the sunlight that shone towards me and for a brief moment, realized that I was in a place that no human should ever be. We are a ground species. We do not fly. Yet here I was, staring face to face with Mother Nature herself. As the sun shone in my eyes, I drank in the blue skies around me. Then looking down expecting to see the ground, I was surprised that all I saw was clouds. *We were above the freaking clouds!* That meant falling through them like a raindrop. We only sat on the edge for a few seconds, but it could have been a lifetime. I couldn't think, I could only feel. It was a blissful state that was unlike anything I had ever experienced. And all I knew was that I wanted it to last forever. With HIM.

And then… just like that, we jumped.

I thought it would be a jump anyway. I had expected to feel gravity pulling us towards the earth at supersonic speed. But it was nothing like what I had expected.

We were freefalling.

Instead of jumping, we simply tilted out of the plane and floated. If we had tumbled forward or backward, I couldn't tell. It was impossible to know if what we were looking at was up or down. I saw sun and sky and clouds one after the other so quickly that my brain couldn't process it. No thoughts, none.

They say the duration is ninety-seconds, but it feels like both the blink of an eye and a lifetime all at once. When you're on the ground, you imagine it will be like that moment before you die. That moment they say your life flashes before your eyes? Except it's not. My mind was void of all thoughts, of all people, of anything at all. Even language ceased to exist in that moment. My brain had literally turned itself off and there was only feeling- exhilaration. For anyone who says that magic doesn't exist, I would challenge to experience the insanity of a ninety-second freefall. It was bliss and heaven and everything in-between. Finally, I felt the tap on my shoulder and it jolted me out of my dream like state as I remembered to open my arms and bend my knees.

Looking down, I saw the clouds approaching and instinctively held my breath as we were about to pass through them. Keeping my eyes open so not to miss anything, I watched as the sun and blue skies disappeared and a murky, dark grey cloud began to surround us. I could feel moisture on my cheeks. It looked like a smoke-filled room, but yet breathing was perfectly easy, no need to hold my breath in at all.

In just a few seconds, the cloud went from dark to light and eventually translucent as we passed through it. Still, I couldn't feel gravity pulling at me. It was like floating with that same weightlessness as being immersed in water.

As the last of the clouds passed us, I began to see an outline of the emerald quilted patchwork below us. I felt myself smile as my world came back in to focus and my brain slowly began to turn back on. Words formed in my head once again, and it was both comforting and sad at the same time.

CASSIDY LONDON

Chapter 8

Dublin, Ireland

Conor Murphy

I checked the altimeter one more time as I placed my hand on the pull cord. I had about five seconds left before I had to pull the chute. That meant that in about five to ten seconds, we would be able to speak again and I would know how she felt. I honestly thought that she was going to say her safe word back in the plane, but I had to admit that I was thrilled that she didn't. Then again, she could have been so terrified that she got caught up in it all and hadn't been able to.

Was she crying right now, and I didn't even know it?

With her strapped to my chest, I had no way of seeing her reactions, knowing what she was feeling, or even what her face looked like. All that would come later when I watched back the Go Pro video footage. I had the camera setup on my left wrist. Right now, all I had was hope. But… if I based myself on all the other first-time jumpers, she was most likely okay. She may have hated the entire jump, but I was pretty sure she was at least alright. She hadn't passed out anyway. She would have gone limp and her head would be slumped forward if that had happened. At least I was out of the woods in the worst-case scenario.

I pulled the cord and felt us jerk upwards and back into the sky a few feet. I lifted the visor on my helmet and began adjusting the cords and prepping the handles immediately. Once everything was secure, I checked on her.

"Ava?" I asked tentatively. She turned her face back up at me. A megawatt smile grinned back at me and I exhaled slowly. She seemed fine.

"I need to release the cords a tad- they're too tight. Remember, you will slide a little." She nodded and a split second later, she slid down a few inches, her head now in line with my belly. A tiny scream of shock escaped her as this happened. We were still about 5,000 feet off the ground. Definitely high enough to panic as she felt the harness release.

"It's okay, I got you!" I called out, reassuring her.

"Are the straps too tight?" I shouted. "A bit", she replied, motioning with her thumb and forefinger. She seemed to squirm uncomfortably.

"Let's loosen them a bit." I continued slacking the straps around her thighs. I pulled them lower and away from her shapely arse, moving them more towards her knees, which enabled her to sit in the harness. By the way she was breathing heavily, and her breasts were sticking out beneath the strap, I knew she could barely breathe. I unbuckled the strap from across her chest.

"Better?" I asked. Ava nodded. She was still heaving from the freefall and seemed unable to form words. The parachute was now open above us and we were slowly floating in the air, letting the wind carry us down. Finally, we would be able to talk and I would know what she was thinking. "What did you think?" I asked, holding my breath waiting for the answer.

"Fucking incredible!" She whispered, her eyes glazed over and her lids hooded.

Just how I imagined she would look after a mind-blowing orgasm.

"Want to grab the handles?" I asked, shaking off the tension that seemed to be back again in full force. "Pull left and we'll go right or vice versa." I explained. She did and we began to twist and turn in the air, floating from one side to the other, overlooking the stunning green carpet beneath us.

"It makes us descend faster!" She called out in surprise. "Yes, of course." Was my response. "Then no! No! I don't want it." She continued, passing back the handles to me. "I just want to enjoy the moment…" She trailed off.

My lips curved upwards until my cheeks hurt. She was special, this lass. I gazed at her tied up in the straps and buckles. My mind was immediately imagining her naked beneath the ropes. Making love to her in the air excited me. I floated off into my own imaginary world of what I would do to her, of how I could make her feel. My thoughts were interrupted by her sweet voice.

"I've never felt anything like that before; it was surreal... Is it always like that?" She questioned innocently.

"Every time, lass." *No. Not every time. Not like this with YOU.*

"We will land shortly, make sure to lift your legs on my command." I instructed. "See there?" I pointed. "That is our landing field." Ava began to wave wildly at her friends and the entire group that were cheering for her just below us.

"Guys!" She called out. "I did it! I fucking did it!"

I told her what to do again right before we hit the ground. We descended with ease and made a clean landing, but it didn't matter. We still ended up skidding until we were laying on our backs; her on top of me looking up at the sky. I could smell her hair in my face, fruits and flowers all mashed together, and feel her weight on my body like a blanket. I could have stayed like that forever.

Knowing I had to release her made a fire grow in my belly. "Get up," I grunted. "Happy? You enjoyed?" I heard myself ask roughly like I was rushing her suddenly. She seemed taken aback by my tone and I didn't blame her.

I quickly unbuckled all the straps as her friends came running towards us. She didn't even look back at me before squealing and throwing herself in their arms. She began to cry with happiness as they lead her away. Talking over each other about their stories as young lasses would. My age seemed to betray me, watching them go. They looked so young and carefree.

With every second that passed I was losing her. Her confidence was back, her excitement at sharing this thrilling experience with her friends. Everything she had needed from me was now lost. I was no longer significant. I knew I was losing, and it frustrated the heck out of me.

I was bent down collecting the equipment when I heard thumping in the grass, making me look up. She had come running back. "Thank you, Conor." She breathed out in-between breaths, grabbing my shoulder for support and staring right into my eyes. "I couldn't have done it without you." Then she leaned in and kissed my cheek.

I growled and nodded. *Why the fuck had she done that?* She could have just walked away with her friends. The end. Such sweetness would have been easier to forget had she disappeared. But she didn't. She showed me something I was not accustomed to… Something softer and sweeter than I had ever known.

She was going to be a hard one to forget, this Ava Jackson.

Chapter 9

Dublin, Ireland

Ava Jackson

As we boarded the bus back to our hotel, I felt a sense of loss or emptiness. I had just lived through the greatest experience of my life, but the one person who had lived it with me, I would never see again. I felt sad that I hadn't experienced it with my girls. Yet I knew in my soul that Conor was the only one able of getting me to follow through with it. With anyone else, I would have backed out. Being grateful didn't even begin to describe my feelings for what he had done for me.

"Avaaaaa!" Called out Sam as she moved back over to sit next to me. "So?" she nudged me. Spill it sister!"

"What?" I asked, as if I didn't understand her.

"I need to know everything! What was it like being with *HIM*?"

"Being with him? Really Sam, you are insinuating something that is totally crazy."

"Is it though?" She mocked me. "You're the one who just jumped to that conclusion, not me!" We both laughed uncontrollably, still giddy from this crazy experience.

"Tell me you didn't think about it though?" She pressed on.

"My guy was hot, too!" Chimed in Adriana as she leaned over from the seat in front of us. "But I'll admit, not like Mr. Green Eyes! Did he even realize that it was us from the airport?"

"I asked, but he said he didn't." I told their disappointed faces.

"Look, the jump was awesome. So much better than I ever expected it could be. And thank goodness he was so professional because I was on the verge of wimping out the whole time."

"What kept you going? Because at one point, I was sure you were going to bail." Adri nudged me as she spoke. "Was it his dreamy eyes or his killer biceps?"

"Very funny... He kept me calm and he suggested that I use a safe word."

Sam and Adri looked at each other, their eyes widening in surprise and jaws dropping. "What?" They screamed before convulsing into laughter and practically sliding off their seats. "What? Like a BDSM safe word? Ava... did he whip you with his belt? Is that how he got you off the plane?" They were officially shaking with laughter now, and egging each other on.

"No... maybe just before he forced her to jump, she

was screaming "No! No!", but because she didn't say–" They waited to hear the word. "Pineapple." I whispered sheepishly. "Because she never said pineapple, he fucking pushed her out!" Adriana shrieked.

"What about mango?" Sam asked in a very serious face. "What if you fucked up and said mango? Would that count? Or would he think you just wanted a mango?"

They were giggling like fools and I wanted to punch them in the face. "It wasn't anything like that at all." I answered as I rolled my eyes and turned to look out the window. I was annoyed with my friends. They were acting childish and immature and it was pissing me off. Granted, I too had thought the idea of a safe word was silly at first. But when I was in the plane and I had to think if I wanted to say it or not, it made sense to me why he had suggested it. It was a way to bypass emotion and really think about your answer.

"Whatever girls, I'm wiped out. I need a nap." I told my friends as I turned to curl up into the window, forming my sweater into a makeshift pillow.

Adri's voice was softer now. "Sorry babe."

"Happy you did it though, Ava." Sam whispered as they both changed seats to hang out with the rest of the noisy crowd in the back of the bus.

I was exhausted all of a sudden. I felt tired all the way

into my bones, and I didn't know why. Maybe because it was like coming down off an intense high. I felt emotional, exhausted, and just wanted to curl up into a ball and sleep in peace. I must have drifted in and out throughout the entire bus ride, because when the bus stopped with a jerk, I nearly fell off my seat. It was dark outside and I was disoriented. Rubbing my eyes, I saw my friends come back up to my seat. "Hey, sorry about before." They said looking sheepish. "We were a bit out of control. Didn't mean to upset you, girl."

"It's okay... maybe I was being over emotional anyway. I was exhausted. I really needed that nap."

"Good! So, you'll be ready to party tonight then?" They questioned, looking like they were both ready to get into trouble. "Why? What's tonight?" I asked sleepily and yawning.

"Oh, you didn't hear the announcement?" Sam asked. "Guess not. I was sleeping remember?" They nodded and laughed. "They're giving us an hour to get ready, then— it's dinner followed by a pub crawl in Dublin tonight."

"Oh wow…"

"Yep, what a way to celebrate the fact that we jumped out of a fucking plane today!" They both cried in unison.

"I've got to admit…" I agreed as I stood up and

grabbed my bags. "We're fucking rock stars!" There was cheering, fist pumping, and high fiving as we skipped off the bus.

We headed to our rooms at the hotel. All three of us were sharing one room. It was crowded, but with the epitome of a girl's slumber party. The perfect way to travel.

"All right girls, let's sex it up tonight! After dinner, we each need to zero in on a hot guy either from the trip or from the pub, but the goal tonight is to hook up!" Said Adriana, the constant party-girl. Sam and I exchanged uncertain glances.

"What are the chances that all three of us find someone the same night?" I asked. "Can we try for something slightly more realistic?"

"Like what?" Adri demanded, throwing her long silky black mane over her shoulder, slightly miffed that I hadn't taken to her suggestion.

"Well… like three different guys buying us all our drinks might be a better place to start." I offered.

"Okay fine, let's start with that." She agreed half-heartedly.

"What about a points system?" I suggested.

"OH YES!" Sam slammed her hand down on the nightstand.

We chatted as we got ready and finally came up with a plan.

Free drinks -5 points
Kissing -10 points
Anything in between -15 points
Sex -20 points

"What does the winner get?" Asked Samantha.

"How about a hundred-dollar shopping spree, financed by the other two in the European city of your choosing?" Adriana suggested.

Sam slammed her hand down on the table. "Done bitches!"

Adri slapped hers over Sam's, "Double done."

I waited, looked around, and shrugged my shoulders. "Let's up the stakes... any guy from the tour is only worth an extra ten points because everyone here is trying to hook up. But a guy from the bar... a local? A guy like that is worth twenty points. You know... just to keep it interesting." I suggested.

"Hell yes!" The girls cheered.

"One... two... three... GO!" We yelled together as we raised our hands in the air.

Game on.

Chapter 10

Dublin, Ireland

Conor Murphy

I barely got through the rest of the day. After Ava and her tour group left, it was one private group after another. Thank God, because it kept me busy and kept my mind off of the craziness of the morning. *Ava.* I couldn't believe it. A man like me should have had more control than that. I let myself get sloppy in her presence. I had been distracted. I'd broken my own cardinal rules, and it could have ended badly... for both of us. I was disgusted with myself. I had fired Dunn for being hung over and unable to focus, yet, I had let myself behave the same way.

Even now, though I was home in my converted loft style attic, visions of her haunted me. What was it about this delicate creature that stirred something inside me that had been dormant for far too long? It's not that I hadn't been around women, lord knows I took my share whenever I wanted. In this town, there were always new faces. Tourists were a dime-a-dozen plus the local girls. Although, if truth be told, I had already sampled most of them... multiple times. But Ava was different, younger than my typical type sure, but that wasn't the only thing. It was the way she looked at me. Made me feel like she saw through the mess and chaos to a secret part of me I kept under lock and key. *Jesus, I sounded like a woman with stupid thoughts.*

Glancing at my watch, I saw that it was getting close to nine o'clock. Definitely pub time. I took a quick shower and changed into civilian clothes. Even after all these years out of the military, I still called anything but my daily uniform of black cargo pants and t-shirt civilian clothes.

Civilian to me meant jeans and a black t-shirt. Not much different I suppose. Either way, I organized my things and set off. Shutting the door to the loft behind me, I wondered if I should have bothered cleaning up Leaving things in a mess was not my typical style, but tonight I didn't care.

As I walked down the cobblestone street towards the pub, my mind wandered back to Ava. I'd probably never see her again. Just the fact I'd seen her twice was on "replay" in my mind. Tonight would be about pints of Guinness beer and checking out some new prospects. I walked into "Ye Ol' Watering Hole" and headed straight for the bar. My spot was there, waiting for me. The bartender, my old friend Eoghan, saw me come through the door and nodded in my direction before sliding a Guinness across the bar. It landed perfectly right in front of me. I smiled as I slid into the stool.

"Eoghan!" I held my pint up and nodded in his

direction. He nodded back, but was still pouring drinks for a rowdy group of American tourists at the other end of the bar.

As Americans usually did in my town, they tried to drink as many beers as they typically did back home. Except for the few who knew strong beer, those boys had been brought up on watered-down versions like Budweiser, Coors, and Miller. The Canadians could last a little longer as they came from a stronger beer country, but no one could rival drinking like an Irishman.

If I was a betting man, I'd say they'd be shitfaced in under an hour.

Eoghan came over to join me moments later. "So, mate?" He asked. "Looks like it's been a rough one today?"

I nodded again. Eoghan knew almost everything about me. He was a good friend and had been for many years. He could read me like no one else. He was also the owner of the place and I respected him as a local fellow business man. We exchanged pleasantries but soon got into the details. As I talked about Ava, I noticed a strange tingling sensation come over my body. Like my blood was warming in my veins. *Had the Guinness been stronger than usual?*

Eoghan kept popping in and out of our conversation

as he served his other clients. About an hour later, two other bartenders showed up to help him out. The pub was getting busier and the heat inside the bar was rising as were the sounds. Drunk people are loud mother-fuckers. I scanned the room for potential women to take my mind off of Ava, but nothing caught my eye. Motioning to Eoghan to pour me another beer, I got up to go to the toilet. That's when I saw the fight that was breaking out. *Typical.*

Eoghan had quickly moved towards it and I caught his eye, silently asking if he needed me to jump in. I often stepped in to help him out in these situations. My days of street fighting could still come in handy for a good cause at least. Eoghan waved me away though, seemed like he had it under control. I held up two fingers to let him know I'd be back in two minutes, and I headed towards the toilet. It was in the back down a long hallway full of memento's, and graffiti on the walls of many moons of tourists. As I turned the corner next to the women's bathroom, I heard what sounded like a whimper. Almost like a frightened dog out in a storm. Something about the sound pulled at my conscience and hit me hard.

"I know what you want, y'a little slut–" Said a gruff voice dripping with contempt. "You were flirting with me all night, little bitch. Now you have the nerve to tell me y'er not interested?!"

The whimpering started again.

"You like that, don't you? You're a dirty little whore. That's it, don't change your tune now, bitch!"

The voice stopped me in my tracks. I heard a slapping sound. He had hit her.

And then I heard a familiar voice. It was *HER* voice. Muffled and slurred, but it was definitely hers. "Please, please don't. I'm sorry... I." Unmistakably her from the way she said "please" to me before the jump.

Blood boiled in my veins instantly as if it were about to explode inside me. I practically smashed open the door to the women's toilet and nearly hurled at the sight on the floor.

It was her– Ava... That fiery auburn hair, wild and tangled, half stuck to her face with tears. Mascara running from her eyes. Her clothes were disheveled, her skirt pushed up around her waist. Her panties... exposed. *I shouldn't even be looking.*

She was crying but half-conscious, slumped on the floor while a brute about half my size with his pants down around his knees kneeled next to her, trying to shove his dick into those ruby quivering lips. I flew into a blind rage.

Grabbing him by the back of his shirt, I pulled him off the ground as his pants slid even further down to his ankles, his belt buckle clashing onto the floor. This miserable, pathetic excuse-of-a-man pleaded for his life. Blubbering even before my fist made contact with his face.

"What the FUCK do you think y'er doing, arshole?" I growled at him. "This is how you treat a woman? She's not your little fuck-toy you bloody dickwad!" I yelled as I pounded into his stomach. With every punch, I could feel my rage intensifying. Beating him was not suppressing it but firing me up even more. Blood seeped out of his nose and mouth and I felt his body go limp as I pushed him up against the wall. He was still blubbering and moaning as he slumped forward, dropping to the floor as I let him go. It was enough. I needed to rein-in my emotions so I could help Ava. But FUCK, I wanted to kill this bastard!

I looked down at her, barely conscious and still whimpering on the ground. Kneeling down next to her, I quickly adjusted her clothing, pulling down that ridiculously short miniskirt and adjusting her tank top. "It's okay sweetheart, you're alright. He won't hurt you anymore." I said as I helped her to her feet. She leaned on me and I put my arm around her for support. I wasn't sure she had seen me or even realized it was me. Her left eye was bruised and her right only half open. Although she reeked of alcohol, it was hard to tell if she was drunk or half-conscious from being hit. Other than a small amount of blood that trickled down her leg, and had probably been from being pushed to the ground, she didn't seem to have any other injuries.

Nothing more visible that I could see anyway. Her panties had looked intact and in place, so she likely had not been raped. My guilt of looking subsided as the instinctive reason I had looked longer than I should have had become perceptible. That put my mind at ease a little more.

"C'mon honey, let's get you back to your group." I would have preferred to call the police, but I knew that would get her nowhere. In this town, the police were most likely out drinking themselves.

I took a step forward, and she slumped over. I had about a second to grab her before she hit the floor for the second time that night.

"Ava? Ava?" I called her name and tapped her cheek gently. Nothing; no response. I scooped her up and marched back out into the bar with her in my arms. Her tiny body was light as a feather, just like when we had jumped. Holding her close like this reminded me of how she had been tied to my body during our jump. Her warm soft curves so close to me was igniting something deep inside me. Not the lust I felt earlier today, but something different– something new. Something protective. I wanted to kill the guy who had touched her– hurt her. *She was mine and I would keep her safe.*

I marched back out into the bar and stood shocked for a second at the sight before me. The bar had somehow cleared out. *Where the fuck was everyone?* It had been buzzing with people and a brewing fight just moments ago.

Eoghan came running over when he saw me. "Jesus man! Where have you been? Could have used the help after all."

Then he looked down at the limp, beautiful, and now lightly snoring girl in my arms.

"Really man? That isn't your style Conor…" He looked at me sideways.

"Fuck off, of course not." I answered, irritated at his insinuation. "Found her in the bathroom, half-conscious and getting attacked by some arsehole, trying to shove his dick in her mouth." I spat.

"Oh feck, tell me you didn't kill the bastard in my bar Con…"

"Eoghan! Give me some credit bub! Granted, he won't be going anywhere soon either. I'm sorry to leave you with that mess." I said, motioning to the toilet. "But this little lass needs to get back to her tour group. The bus is outside?" I asked as I walked towards the front of the bar.

"Uh, no man, that tour bus got the feck out of here when the riot started. They rounded up all their people and took right off."

"WHAT? They left her?" I was in shock.

"Uh… don't know mate. Look let me check on the bastard you beat up, and then we'll figure out what to do with her." Eoghan said as he ducked into the back.

"Feck Conor, I had enough of a mess already tonight without you knocking a man unconscious!" He called out, frustrated. "Bring me some ice!"

I felt for my friend, and under normal circumstances, I'd have helped him into the wee hours of the morning, but Ava needed me more right now. The poor lass had been assaulted and abandoned. I needed to call around. I lay her down across the bar. She was sleeping now, lightly snoring as her chest heaved up and down. She curled up on her side and I was glad to see her move on her own. She needed to sleep off that drink, though. I wondered how many she had downed into that tiny body. As she curled up tighter, her breasts pushed together, spilling a touch out of her top, accentuating her already beautiful cleavage. Even drunk and roughed up, she was perfect.

Shaking the thoughts from my head, I picked up my phone and called the local motel that typically housed the tour groups. That meant talking to Molly. Thankfully, things weren't awkward with her, despite having fucked her behind the front desk of the motel on more than one occasion.

"Hello, Motel 6. Molly speaking. How can I help you?"

"Molly, it's Conor. I have a girl here at Eoghan's place who missed her bus and needs to rejoin her group."

"Conor... Are you picking up drunken tourists again? You know you don't have to babe, I'm always here when you need a little fun." She teased.

Molly was a tease and a quick lay when it was needed, but I was in no mood to flirt with her tonight. "Mols, this can't wait... please?" I asked.

"Sorry Con, you'll have to keep her for the night. That bus checked out earlier this evening. From what I heard, they were doing a late-night trip up to Belfast."

FUCK ME!

This was not good. Ava was hurt, drunk, and passed out in a foreign city and had now been abandoned by her group. I rarely took care of drunk tourists, even beautiful girls like her. So why I even felt it was my responsibility gnawed at my brain. Yet still... she was a helpless young girl who had been taken advantage of. And in this moment, her safety and security resided with me and me alone.

I left her sleeping on the bar and took the ice over to Eoghan. "Looks like we have two boarders tonight aye?" He laughed as he packed the ice and handed it to the arsehole who had now woken up and was sitting up, leaning on the wall.

"YOU! You're the fucker who attacked me!" He cried.

"Y'er lucky, I didn't kill y'a, you stupid whanker!" I spat.

"She wanted it; was flirting with me all night." He muttered.

"Yeah?" I was fuming. "Because when I found her, she was half-passed out, half-cryin', had been hit, and you were trying to shove your lousy miniscule dick in her mouth!"

Eoghan got between me and the guy just as I was about to knock him senseless for the second time that night. "Okay mate, I'll take care of him, you figure out what to do with the miss."

"Yeah, I'm taking her home to sleep it off. Then I'll help her reconnect with her group in the morning."

"Seriously?" Eoghan just looked at me. "You're taking her home? Not the motel?"

"I would, but her group checked out and left for Belfast. I spoke to Molly."

"Well feck– what will she think of that when she wakes up at your place, mate?"

"Hopefully, only good things. Don't have much of a

choice anyway." I responded, shrugging my shoulders.

"Okay, keep in touch Conor."

"You too, Eoghan."

Back at the bar, I placed some ice into a bar towel for Ava, then scooped her up in my arms. I smiled to myself as she snuggled into my chest. Her hair had fallen gently over her face and her fingers wrapped around the collar of my shirt. *This day was getting crazier by the minute.*

The streets were empty and silent. Only the sound of my boots could be heard on the cobblestone street. I felt Ava shiver and moan as the air hit her skin. I held her tighter against me. The makeshift icepack was not helping.

It's okay sweetheart, I'll take care of you.

My thoughts fucking scared the shit out of me, almost as much as the raging hard-on inside my jeans.

Chapter 11

Dublin, Ireland

Ava Jackson

Light appeared from behind my eyelids, turning my brain onto unfamiliar sounds. As I listened, I tried to place the sounds I heard, but nothing made sense. Sounds of a busy kitchen and classical music filled my ears and raised questions in my mind. As busy as my brain was trying to figure it out, my body felt paralyzed. Even consciously thinking about moving hurt for the first couple of minutes as I drifted in and out of this strange half-awake, half-asleep consciousness.

Finally, I pried open my eyes and my gaze focused in on a ceiling above me. It was white with beams in brown wood, slanted like in an attic. I didn't recognize it and pushed my head up on my elbows to get a better look of my surroundings.

Where the FUCK am I? My head spun as I looked around, panic shrouding me like a heavy blanket.

I was still drunk, that much I knew for sure. The room was spinning and I was still lying down. I knew that feeling, but something else was wrong. I was in a comfortable loft-like room, in a king-size bed with a dresser and a window. None of which was familiar in the least. Wherever I was, I had never been there before. And to make it worse, I did not understand how I'd gotten there. A glass of water was on the table next me. I reached for it and gulped most of it back before panicking as to perhaps if it was laced with poison. I needed to know where I was and what the hell had happened last night. And I needed to know now.

"Sam? Adri?" My voice sounded muffled and my throat was hoarse and dry.

As I pushed myself up to sit and swing my legs out of the bed, I had yet another heart attack. I was wearing nothing but an oversized white t-shirt and my underwear... *Where were my clothes?* Tears stung my eyes as I stood up, grabbing the headboard for support as I stumbled from my spinning head.

Oh, my God... Someone must have drugged me last night! Think Ava! What was the last thing I remembered?

My first thought was of how the girls and I had danced on the bar, being silly and careless. And the drinks—ohhh... the drinks. We had done so many shots... My hands cupped my face in despair. The guys... the dancing... grinding... our stupid fucking bet! So fucking stupid! Then a vision of the bathroom flew into my head.... My hands flew to my mouth to stop the scream from escaping. *The guy, the guy in the bathroom! Oh My God! He must have kidnapped and raped me and now*

I'm his prisoner in this place! I looked around the room wildly.

My mind was on overdrive and panic blurred my vision. I couldn't breathe. The room was getting smaller, but I couldn't give in. I had to fight. I had to save myself and get the fuck out of here. *Weapon! Find something to use…*

I sat on the side of the bed and dropped my head between my knees as I tried to ward off the impeding darkness overtaking me. But it was too late, black dots were coming fast and with no mercy for me, from behind my head. They were threatening to cloud my vision completely. I heard the door open and heavy footsteps march into the room. Looking up quickly, the glass of water still in my hand, I threw it in the direction of the steps. *Please let it hit him, please let it hit him.* I prayed as I felt myself succumbing to the blackout and falling to the ground.

The ice-cold temperature woke me abruptly. My eyes opened and confusion hit me instantly. *Was I still under?* I thought as I looked into the concerned face of a very attractive man. Shaggy hair was hanging over his eyes tickling my nose. Ink ran up the lengths of his huge arms, and those eyes… Oh my God, those eyes. Immediately, I knew where I had seen that emerald before. I jumped up and scrambled on to the bed, hugging a pillow to my chest, squatting on my knees.

"YOU! I know you!" I cried, my voice hoarse and strained with fear.

"Fuck! What have you done? Back the hell away from me, you psycho!" I shrieked, overwhelmed with terror.

"Ava, please! You have every right to be scared, but please let me explain." He said, his hands up in surrender as he took a few steps back.

"Why should I? Looks like you fucking kidnapped me!" Tears welled up in my eyes as I felt myself shake uncontrollably. I pointed accusingly at him.

"You should thank me for saving you from a worst fate, lass." He said in a calm and controlled manner.

"What do you mean?" I asked slowly, my voice a little steadier this time. Conor kept his distance on the other side of the room, which allowed me to breathe a little.

"What's the last thing you remember from the bar?" he asked.

"Uh… dancing, and drinking with my friends…" I muttered.

"You don't remember what happened in the toilet? I found you with a man…" Conor continued.

That's when even more came flooding back. The dancing, the drinks, the hands under my skirt on the dance floor. I sank back into the pillows with dread in

106

my heart. "I remember going to the bathroom, but not much of what happened after that."

Conor sighed. "Can I sit?" he asked as he motioned towards the bed. I nodded, already feeling safer than I had only moments ago.

"I found you on the floor of the toilet with a man who had his hands all over you. He had already hit you and pushed you around. A moment or two later and it would have been much worse."

Holy fuck… I remembered it clearly. Hands in places I didn't want them to be, a pain in my head… black-and-white tiles on the floor…

"He must have roofied my drink… Thank you for saving me, but… my clothes? My friends?" I questioned. "Why am I here?" I pressed, crossing my arms over my chest, all too aware of my nakedness beneath the t-shirt.

"Ah yes, your clothes… I apologize for that, but you had vomited all over yourself. I didn't want you to sleep like that so I…."

"You undressed me?" My voice croaked and filled with embarrassment. The man I had lusted after yesterday had seen my naked body… my vomit filled naked body.

Staring down at his feet and refusing to look up, he

said, "I didn't look. I did what needed to be done. Same as I would have done for my sister."

I said nothing more about it. "Does anyone know where I am? I have to call the tour guide!"

"Yes, you will need to do all that but just so you know, I brought you here because your bus left last night. Checked out of the motel and left to their next destination. Belfast, I believe."

My heart sank. They had left? This confirmed that all of it had really happened. They had warned us that if anyone missed the bus along the way, that it was our responsibility to find it again. Tour busses wouldn't wait for anyone, they said. It had even been in the waiver.

I was fucked.

"My cell phone?" I asked, searching through the blankets.

"You didn't have one on you. I checked. You didn't even have a purse and absolutely nothing in your pockets."

My head was buzzing with pain. "Why does my head hurt so much?" I muttered.

"Well, for one, you have a nasty hangover, but two, that arsehole in the bar seemed to have hit you in the head. You were bleeding when I found you. I put ice on it, but I'm not surprised it still hurts."

"What happened to him?" I asked quietly.

"He's worse off than you this morning, trust me." Conor smirked to himself, looking away.

I smiled. Conor seemed to be a stand-up guy. Not to mention that the pain in my head didn't stop me from noticing that he was even more gorgeous in this relaxed setting.

Jesus, you have no time to chat Ava.

I had no money, no identification, no phone, and no fucking idea where my tour was. *Should I go to the police? Call the tour company? My dad back home?*

Conor stood up. "Listen Ava… I washed your clothes." He said as he handed me my clothes from last night, now clean and folded. "There's a shower in the adjoining room. Get yourself ready while I make us some food. Then you can call the tour company and see where they will head to next. I'll take you there myself to join up with them."

"Okay… thanks Conor. Also, Conor?" I asked as he walked out of the room.

He turned back and just like that, warmth washed over me.

"Thank you for last night. I feel like it would have been

a much worse evening for me without you."

He nodded and closed the door behind him.

I looked out the window to get a sense of where I was. The morning dew made everything seem so ghost-like. I turned away sad, mimicking the droplets of dew on the window scurrying down. No place on earth is safe. Not even Ireland with all its gorgeous landscapes... or the men.

I walked into the bathroom, quietly closing the door, and removed the t-shirt he had clothed me with. Staring into a full-length mirror, I looked at my body expecting the worst. Dried blood in my hairline, across my left knee. Dark circles under my eyes, remnants of mascara wiped across my face. Light bruising on the backs of my arms and thighs. It was brutal.

Yet, I trusted Conor. Despite waking up naked in the house of an older man, who could have kidnapped me and made those bruises himself, and despite admitting to undressing me, I was no longer afraid.

Visions of "Misery" by Stephen King played in my head. Except in this version I was the writer, and he was the drop-dead, gorgeous man who had imprisoned me. Not that that was necessarily a bad thing...

Chapter 12

Dublin, Ireland

Conor Murphy

I closed the door gently so I would not scare the poor lass. She was already on the verge of a mental breakdown. I hated myself for undressing her last night, but since I had not involved police or the hospital, I had to make sure she was ok. God knows my military training included some experience in attending to the injured. It was a duty to make sure she had nothing serious going on beneath her clothes… I could see in her eyes that she was wondering whether I was telling the truth about the man in the toilet. I could see the mistrust and I was kicking myself for it. I hadn't been thinking last night. I had been worked up. I needed to regain my self-control.

She was here. Ava. And she was half naked in my guest bedroom. When she had sat up, her breasts had swung from side to side gently, her nipples poking through the sheer worn out white fabric. I could almost feel their weight in my hands as they moved, and imagined my thumbs rubbing those sensitive nipples to a stiff peak. I wanted to suckle them so badly. The ache in my pants suddenly jolted me back to reality.

Fuck me. What was I thinking? This was a sick scenario.

She was terrified and lost. Her eyes had looked at me with complete helplessness as she had gripped the pillow to her chest tightly.

What if she went to the police? There was no proof I hadn't been the one to harm her. I could only hope I could show her that wasn't the case. Eoghan would have to testify on my behalf.

I needed to keep my hands busy to keep my mind off the situation, so I cooked. I'd been on my own since my teens and had always enjoyed a good meal. I took out the eggs, sausages, hash, and tomatoes, and started the fry-up.

I heard soft footsteps padding along the floor and I turned. Ava stood there, her hair wet from the shower and her face scrubbed clean. Tiny freckles spattered across her nose. Those soft caramel eyes seemed calmer now. I breathed a sigh of relief at her new sense of relaxation. She seemed slightly self-conscious though, as she pulled at her short mini skirt. In the light of day, I could tell that the clothes that made her feel sexy last night were now a source of discomfort despite them being clean.

"Can I get you a jumper?" I asked, trying hard to not stare at her stunning cleavage and those perfectly curved hips that looked as if they had melted into the skirt.

"Uh… what?" She questioned.

I laughed. "A sweater, I think you would call it?"

"Oh… umm, sure. I'd like that." She laughed.

I threw her a plaid utility shirt that was on the back of a chair. "You can keep this." I said as I tossed it to her.

Despite it shrinking in the dryer recently, she still had to roll the sleeves and tie up the bottom. She looked fucking sexy as hell in my old shirt, making it practically impossible to keep myself in check.

"Here..." I said. "Sit down and eat, you must be starving."

Her eyes softened, and she smiled more as she sat down.

Silence filed the room as we ate, neither one of us able to look the other in the eye.

I had to put an end to this uncomfortable mess. "Maybe you want to call someone after you eat?" I suggested.

"Yes! I will call the tour group and see what they suggest I do. And… unfortunately, I will have to call my dad, too. He may need to wire me some money." She said between bites. "Everything was pre-paid for us so I left my wallet in my purse on the bus." She said, chewing her lip.

I barely heard her words. All I could see were her lush pink lips, so full, flushed with color and juicy as she continuously ran her tongue across them. I wanted to sink my teeth into her, suck on that lower lip until she cried out. I wanted to fuck her mouth, her beautiful mouth, with my tongue. I couldn't stop the mass of dirty thoughts from penetrating my head.

This girl was making me crazy. I needed her out of my place before I did something I would regret.

"Conor?" She blurted out, looking up and staring deep into my eyes. She flipped her hair absently, which was drying with natural waves in it, and let her hand trail down her collarbone, resting on her lap. I noticed a pink blush creep up across the bare skin of her chest, her breasts raising and lowering with each breath. *Was she nervous? Or was it something else?*

I could swear her nipples were swelling through her shirt, but her eyes seemed worried and her face anxious. All I wanted to do was pull her into my arms, straddle her over my lap on this chair, and hold her tight. Tell her I'd take care of her while caressing her sweet plump ass. *Fuck!* This shit had to stop. She would never be interested in a man like me and I needed no one to tell me that I wasn't good for her. I knew that already.

She reached across the table and put her tiny hand in mine. It was warm and soft and I had to hold back from bringing it to my lips. *Had I been reading her wrong?*

Her lips trembled and her eyes filled with tears.

"I'm sorry Ava, I know you're scared… but I promise I won't hurt you. I…"

"Conor… it's not that at all. Actually, I trust you. I'm just nervous because I know I have to call my dad. He will totally kill me!" Her head dropped into her hands and her hair fell forward.

She trusts me. She trusts me. Oh, little one, you don't even know me. Said my brain as my heart jumped over itself in leaps and bounds.

"Well, for sure he won't be too happy, but he will help you, right?" I asked, trying to stay on track with the conversation.

"Yes, but it's just that he wasn't keen for me to go on this trip, and he warned me about going places alone and never being without my money or passport. So… when he hears I did all the things he warned me against, he's going to seriously kill me. He may just cut my trip short and make me go home." She bowed her head in shame.

Without thinking, I reached out and grabbed her wrist, pulling her closer to me. She scooted forward in her chair, which hiked her skirt a little higher. Her bare thighs were below my field of vision. Her eyes were still red and worry was painted all over her pretty face. But something else, too. We stared at each other without speaking for several minutes. I watched as her eyes traveled across my face, to my chest, my arms, and lower down.

My cock pushed angrily against the zipper of my jeans. She had to have noticed. My bulge was obvious. This time I heeded his call and broke yet another rule.

I pulled Ava's hand closer, until it was over my chest. My legs spread open so she could come closer to me. Her face now inches from mine, I could feel her warm breath, her sweet scent calling my body to it. She leaned in closer, her breath pulling me into her. It was there and we could both feel it. *Desire. Passion.* Our bodies called to each other. I had to take the chance. Worst case, she would change her mind and leave, but at least I would have tasted her.

Grabbing the back of her head quickly, I pulled her in and kissed her hard. That pink lower lip of hers that has been tempting me was just as juicy as I had imagined. I could feel her initial surprise when I pulled her in, but she softened within seconds, molding to my touch. Her body instinctively let go under my command. She was everything I had imagined and more. I knew in that moment I would never let her go.

Chapter 13

Dublin, Ireland

Ava Jackson

At first, I wasn't sure. I had been so preoccupied with being left behind and dealing with my hung-over body and mind that I hadn't seen it coming.

Initially, it angered me that he hadn't gone to the police and he assumed undressing me was okay. I felt exposed and humiliated and honestly, just stupid. I had made so many mistakes in such a short period of time.

Conor was a vision of perfect masculinity and it was as distracting as ever. Those broad shoulders and back, his chest and biceps rippling with muscles every time he moved. I remembered how he had tightened the straps on my harness and how he held me close right before the jump, calming my mind and spirit.

Every time he spoke, his accent alone made me wet my panties. He seemed to fight an internal battle as much as I did. I just had no idea it was desire, until he kissed me.

His kiss was forceful and brutish and it ignited a fire in my blood that I had never felt before. This was a man who didn't ask, he took what he wanted. He had taken me from the club and now taken me with this kiss. A buzz shot through my veins and tingled into my nipples and between my legs. My body was sore from last night, but this adrenaline rush seemed to numb the pain. For all his force, he was also gentle. As if once he took what he wanted, he coaxed pleasure out of me. Consent coming through a split second behind my body's betrayal.

He released my lips with a pop, the cold air shocking them after the warmth of his mouth. We stared into each other's eyes without moving, and breathing heavily, he said, "Call your father and then we will figure out how to get you where you need to be." He slid his cell phone to me as if the kiss had never happened.

Still shaken from his touch, I picked up the phone and dialed home. My dad picked up on the first ring. "Babycakes!" his voice called out. "Hang on a second, I've got the top down on the car. It's windy." He said, adjusting the connection.

"It's okay Daddy, I can hear you!" I called back, trying to sound chipper.

"How's the trip so far?" My dad asked.

"Um... okay. Well, it was amazing until something happened."

"Ava... Are you okay? What happened?" His voice was now filled with concern.

"I missed the bus!" I sobbed. The sobs came out harder and harder until I could barely get a word out.

"Ava? Ava? Talk! Where are you? Where are you calling from? Where are your friends?"

My dad's questions were like a firing squad aimed right at my heart. I hated to disappoint him. My mom had done that enough over the years. She was twelve years younger than my dad and was vocal about how marriage and motherhood stifled her. She was always disappearing for days before returning to us without so much as an explanation. It was a constant event in my life until I was ten years old. That last time, she left and never came back.

Since then, it had been my dad and I. Fortunately, he worked for the government and could provide all the luxuries life could offer, but nothing was a replacement for a mother. Even his love, which was all-encompassing and often overbearing, wasn't enough. I loved being Daddy's girl, but it still didn't fill the hole in my heart that my mother should have.

Which was why disappointing him was so heartbreaking. I had worked so hard to get him to agree to this trip and now here I was, fucking it up just as he had feared.

Just then, Conor grabbed the phone out of my hand.

"Hello there, Sir." He began formally.

"Who the fuck are YOU?" Came my dad's rage-filled voice from across the ocean. "What the fuck have you done to my daughter? If you laid one finger on my daughter, I will kill you, you bastard!"

"Calm down Mr...." Conor looked at me quizzically, silently asking my last name. "Jackson" I mouthed to him silently.

"Mr. Jackson, stop screaming and listen." He said forcefully. "I fully understand your concern, but know that I have helped your daughter and not harmed her." Conor then put the speakerphone on so I could hear and interject.

"It's true dad, he's been good." I answered meekly, still reeling from both Conor's kiss and his reaction to my dad.

Conor quickly explained what had happened last night. My dad yelled again as soon as he heard about my drinking. "Calm down, Mr. Jackson. It serves no purpose to yell at Ava now. I agree that her behavior was reckless, but what's done is done."

"Anyway, like I said, bringing her here was my only option last night. But today I will ensure that she gets back on with the tour. She needs some of your financial help I believe though…" Conor passed the phone back.

"Dad?" I whispered. Silence. "I'm sorry Dad."

"I'm wiring money as soon we get off the phone. Get out of there now Ava, and get to the closest hotel. Any man who takes you home to his place is not looking out for your best interest, no matter what he says. I'll send the money and contact the tour group and the embassy about your passport. I'm aiming for twenty-four hours max until I can get you on a plane. You can forget this stupid vacation."

I didn't answer... I had no words.

"Understood?" My dad repeated.

All I could do was mumble a halfhearted "Yes..." before the line went dead.

I watched frozen as Conor began to slowly clear the breakfast dishes. He casually walked over to the sink and washed the dishes by hand. In silence.

Bile was coming up in my throat. This couldn't be happening. I had fucked everything up. My dad had freaked out and although I was pissed that he wanted me back home, I also couldn't blame him. I had been stupid. I had no money and no passport and was alone in a foreign county with a skydiving instructor I barely knew. A man, who in the last twenty-four hours, had protected my life at fourteen-thousand feet, saved me from an attack and possible assault, undressed me, and had kissed me like I'd never been kissed before.

It confused me and felt like I couldn't distinguish good

from bad or right from wrong anymore. The only thing I knew was that I wanted so desperately to be held in his strong arms and feel his lips on mine again. Safety and comfort were within my reach, but I wasn't sure I could reach for them.

I hoped he would turn and say something, but he didn't. I don't know how long we stayed like that, but it seemed like an eternity.

Chapter 14

Dublin, Ireland

Conor Murphy

The situation was just infuriating. I had about twenty-four hours before I would lose her entirely. Lose my chance to hold her close to my heart and feel her lush body beneath mine. It was obvious she wanted me too. I knew it for sure now after her response to my impulsive kiss. From that first moment back in New York, to the jump, to her here now. Nothing was just pure chance. The Irish believed in luck yes, but destiny, and fate, was also a huge belief. I believed more than ever now that she and I were meant to meet.

Fuck it. Fuck all of it. If I would lose her, then I would also take the only chance I had to be with her. I could hear her sniffling and sobbing quietly behind me while I decided what to do. Heat was building in my body. My dick was fucking cramping it was so hard for her. I needed her like I needed to breathe. Letting the last dish clatter into the sink, I turned to look at her.

That ridiculously short miniskirt was riding up her thighs exposing nearly everything. I could see her full ass again as I glimpsed her lacy panties beneath it. Her tits were heaving and pushing against my plaid shirt that was tied around her. I walked over and stood in front of her chair.

"Conor, I'm so sorry my dad yelled at you like that."
She began. "I'm so embarrassed. You've done
everything to help me and you didn't deserve that. I am
completely humiliated."

"Ava, it's fine. I probably would have had the same
reaction if I had been in your dad's position. What you
did was reckless, and it put you in a bad position. You
could have been raped last night by that arsehole. I
don't even want to think about what could have
happened if I hadn't found you." I paused, running my
hand through my hair in frustration, but she didn't
move or speak.

"But as you will leave in about twenty-four hours, I also
need you to know something. That kiss earlier was not
a fluke. I've wanted to taste you since the moment I
saw you." Words failed me as her eyes softened and a
blush returned to her cheeks. That was all the consent
I needed.

Cupping her chin in my hand, I raised her to her feet.
She was so small she only reached my chest. I slid my
hands beneath her underarms and lifted her up higher,
encouraging her as she wrapped her legs around my
waist. My hands moved under her to support her in
place. Her soft ass in my hands was enough to drive
me wild as I sucked her tongue deep into my mouth. I
wanted to touch and her taste her all over. I wanted her

naked in my bed. Her skin, soft and moist beneath my touch. I wanted to drink in her lush body and rock her from the inside out until she came all over my cock.

"Come, baby." I murmured as she moaned into me. "I need to take you to bed."

With quick strides across the attic, I got us to my bed in seconds. "I want to look at you." I whispered as I set her down on the bed. I lifted her arms and pulled off her tank top, letting her beautiful breasts pop out. Running my thumbs across her nipples, scraping lightly with my nails, I could feel them harden to my touch beneath her silky lace bra. She was practically moaning, and I had barely touched her. I loved how she said nothing, but had just allowed me to explore her body as if I already owned it. I pushed her mini skirt up around her tiny waist and drank in the sight of her. "Beautiful, so fucking beautiful."

Shit, I would have to take things slow with her, though. She was still young and probably inexperienced with some of the kinkier things I usually favored. That's when the thought hit me. *What if she was a virgin? Nah… not at twenty-two.* Still though, I had to ask. "Ava, are you a virgin, sweetness?" I asked gently between labored breaths as her hands roamed my chest and arms.

She giggled playfully. "Do you want me to be?"

"Ava!" I growled, annoyed at her teasing. "Answer the

question."

"No…" She blushed. "I'm not a virgin but… I've only been with one other guy. And that was in high school. And… he turned out to be gay. So…" Redness covered her chest and face as eyes averted mine.

"Okay… that was high school, but what about college?" I pressed.

"No… that was an even bigger mess." She whispered.

I was incredulous "So, you've been celibate for a few years?"

"Well… you know… I do my thing…" She stared right into my eyes. I understood exactly what she meant.

"Oh, baby…" I murmured as my lips left a trail of kisses across her exposed collarbone. This beautiful, sexually repressed creature was half naked and wriggling with desire on my bed. She had not been touched in years other than a high school boy? This was too good to be true.

"And you don't think I'm too old for you?" I whispered.

"Well, how old are you?" She asked nervously. "Not so old you can't use it, I hope?" she winked.

"I'm thirty-eight, you little minx, and let me show you how well I can use it!" I growled as I grabbed her and flipped her over across my lap. My hands roamed her body, pushing that skirt over her plump arse, exposing her as she instinctively spread her legs apart. She pushed her ass up. *Good girl.* I caressed her back and ass and the length down to her thighs, carefully circling away from her pussy. She looked over her shoulder and I thought I detected a little apprehension in her eyes.

"Uh, what are you doing?" she panted out. Her breathing was becoming labored with simply caressing her in all the right places. I wanted to suck her and taste her so badly.

"I can see that you like to tease, little Ava. Two can play at that game, baby."

Her bra flicked open under one hand as I pulled her panties down with the other. She was now across my knee, naked but for her skirt that was pushed up around her waist. Her panties slipped around her knees, and her beautiful luscious ass was on display. Almost instantly, I felt her beginning to tremble.

"Shhh… I won't hurt you. I like to look at you in this compromising position." I reassured her as my hands rubbed circular patterns along those pretty white ass cheeks. I was stroking her lightly with my fingertips right below the ass cheeks. This was such a sensitive area. I trailed my long fingers around each cheek, and with each round, I inched closer to her freshly waxed pussy I had glimpsed. *Gotta love American girls.*

I spread her ass apart staring at it. Fuck. She was ready for me. I could see glistening on the folds as I spread it further apart, now seeing all of her exposed to me. I blew quickly on her pussy, and released her ass cheeks. I felt her breath hitch again.

I couldn't help myself. "You'll find that I enjoy giving a good spanking or two when the behavior is warranted."

She gasped. "I've never done that before…"

"Does that shock you?" I whispered close to her, still circling my hands around her perfectly plump bottom. "Uh, no… I don't know if I'd like it."

"Fair enough. You can think about that and let me know." I answered as I flipped her over and sat her on my lap. I wanted to enter her now. With my fingers, with my tongue, with my cock. But it was more exciting this way. *Patience Conor– enjoy this while you still can.*

A beautiful sight she was; those huge heavy tits hanging near my face, pink nipples that were perked up to diamond hardness, begging to be sucked. Her soft naked pussy on my lap, her panties now fallen to her ankles. She was fucking stunning, squirming in my lap and trying to hold it in.

"Don't be ashamed, pet… your body knows exactly what it wants. And… I intend to give it to you." My fingers danced up her thigh as the words fell gently

128

from my mouth. It was more than that though... I had known it from the second I saw her, I needed to claim her as my own. Even if she was everything I couldn't have.

I listened to her breath but kept my eyes on hers as my hand slowly pushed between her naked thighs and towards her heated center. She instinctively began to rock back and forth on me as her gaze dropped and my hand inched towards her pink wet lips. "Never do that Ava." I said, lifting her chin. "I want to see you. I want to watch your eyes roll back in your head when I make you come."

Her thighs were now open wider as I slid my fingers across her wet slit. "Ughhh lass, y'er so wet baby... that pretty little cunt of yours is just dripping for me." A moan escaped her lush mouth as she threw her head back at my words and arched for me, gripping my shoulders for support and grinding down on my hand. I delved further into my Irish accent the more aroused I became, much like when I drank. I quickly circled her back with my left arm as she arched even further. I skimmed my fingers across her swollen folds, finally tracing circles around her swollen clit. Ava thrashed in my arms. Those beautiful breasts bounced in front of me for my own pleasure, as my fingers beckoned her towards bliss. My fingers were so wet, they glided with ease in and out of her, and I spread her juices all over her pussy, coating it each time I exited her folds.

"Conor! Oh… please…" She moaned. Her quick reaction made me chuckle. "Pet… this is just the beginning. Make no mistake. I will make you come, but not like this. Not before I taste that sweetness between your legs." I abruptly stopped. She was pent up from years of not being properly fucked. I wanted to control when she would come for me, but she was so wet. It was dripping on my jeans. *FUCK…*

She gasped as I scooped her up into my arms and placed her on the bed. Slowly pulling off her panties that were tied around her ankles, I spread her legs wide and positioned myself between them. I lifted my shirt over my head, throwing it and exposing my entire self to her now. I slacked my belt and quickly unbuttoned my jeans, leaving my cock exposed with my jeans loosely hanging below my Adonis belt. I was not wearing any boxers. My face was now inches from her wet folds. I looked up at her as my tongue tip grazed along her open slit, making her shudder violently. "So sweet, just like the forbidden fruit…" My mouth curved upwards before sinking back down into layers of sweetly scented warmth.

Her hands immediately went to my hair and pulled as I licked and sucked with a vengeance. She spread herself even wider and rocked into my mouth savagely. The moans emanating from her beautiful mouth were enough to drive me wild. I alternated between flicking and sucking her clit until she thrashed wildly under my viciously quick tongue. My dick throbbed, gorged beneath me as I was lying flat on my belly eating her up.

She screamed my name as she came and it was the most beautiful sound I'd ever heard. "So fucking sweet." I murmured, lapping up her juices as they came squirting out. As she relaxed, I pulled myself away from her slowly, trailing kisses down her thighs and spreading her come as I kissed her. Ava lay there shaking before I pulled her into my arms and cradled her, dropping tiny kisses along her neck this time. This woman felt special to me, seemed so different than anyone I'd ever met before. A little fiery and wild angel. I had visions of her being the light to my darkness, although I would never subject her with that burden. That was my cross to bear. This moment with her was all I would ever get, and that was okay. It would have to be.

"Conor…" She whispered, her delicate voice bringing me back to earth.

Her hands ran over my raging hard-on that felt like it was about to explode. I grabbed her hands with a little more force than I intended to, making her jump and her eyes widen. Sliding over to the foot of the bed, I motioned for her to do the same. "Get on your knees, Ava." She scrambled quickly to the floor, her eyes never leaving mine, her pink nipples dancing as she moved. I fucking loved how quickly she followed directions. Her hands were on my crotch instantly, pawing at my jeans. I stood up to allow her to undress the rest of me.

To watch this beautiful woman undress me from her knees, naked, was enough to put me right over the edge. I needed to slow down before I lost control and did too much too soon. Her hands encircled my shaft as she freed it completely, and her eyes widened in appreciation.

"Fuck…" I groaned as her tiny hands stroked me up and down, cupping my balls. This woman would be the end of me.

She smiled as her lips formed an "O" and she reached in closer. Her hot, wet mouth was on me and she slowly took me in, all the way to the back of her throat. "That's it, baby. Take my cock, angel, take it all in." I breathed into her.

Holding onto all the control I had left, I knew I had to take this slow and let her take the reins. I pushed away all thoughts of ramming my cock hard into her mouth until tears would sting her eyes. I let her take control. I allowed her to move as she wished. Shocking this pretty little thing was not on the agenda for tonight.

Ava sucked me so fucking slow. The slower she went, the more I wanted to grab her by the hair, hold her head, and pound myself into that sassy little mouth of hers. But I took my time. I held back.

After a few minutes though, I was done. "Enough!" I growled. Frustrated that I felt the need to hold back, but also fearful that her damn slow sucking might make me come.

"Your hot little mouth will make me come like that, you little minx." I growled as I pulled her warm body into my arms. "Isn't that the point?" she flirted, rolling her eyes at me. She had her hands on my pecks and lazily circled my nipples, nipping me with her nails... *FUCK*. Small things never sent me out of control and over the edge. One touch from her and I could burst in under a millisecond.

"No Ava. It's not." Her eyes squinted at me, questioning.

"When I do come, baby, it won't be anywhere but deep inside your pussy. You know why?" She shook her head slowly. "Because right now, in this moment, you're MINE."

As we rolled back on to the bed, my mouth came down on her perky little nipple hard. I grazed my teeth over that little nub just hard enough to make her squeal again.

My fingers replaced my mouth as I reached over to the nightstand for a condom. Damn how I wanted to slide inside her, our bare flesh connecting. But what my body wanted and what I knew was right were two different things. Even in this moment, my mind and my body were forever at war.

"Are you ready angel?" I whispered. Her pupils dilated with apprehension. "I'll go nice and slow for you, baby." I positioned myself in front of her, spreading her thighs slowly.

She nodded. "I feel slow isn't really your thing though…" Ava teased.

"Still taunting me, are we? Even in the most precarious of situations now?" I laughed

I liked her boldness, her inquisitive mind. The way she poked and questioned my intentions. I liked it all. Just about as much as I liked her naked body beneath me, in front of me, and maybe even tied up for me…

As I showered her soft neck with kisses, I pushed ever so slightly inside her. I pumped my hard tip on her clit, feeling it gorge with blood and harden. Her cunt was hot, wet, and oh… so fucking tight. She tightened her face as she was preparing for the worst. "No, breathe pet, it's okay… this will feel so fucking good I promise." She exhaled slowly and nodded.

"Put your hands in my hair like before." I instructed.

I waited for her to relax and when she did, I pushed in ever so slightly. Feeling her tightness suck my cock inside was torture, but I didn't move. Staying still and letting her get used to the feeling was crucial.

Then, when a smile slowly came across her lips and she began to gently squirm beneath me, I gave her what she needed. I plunged in as far as I could go and her breath hitched. I began sliding my cock in and out of her sweet tight pussy. This was the only place I ever wanted to be. Her cunt milked my cock almost immediately, pulsating again and again. I quickened my pace and pushed harder into her with each stride until she screamed and dug her nails down into my back. I was grunting like a beast. Knowing she came because of me sent me over the fucking moon.

Pushing a strand of hair from her face, I smiled. "So fucking beautiful, Ava. I could watch you come all fucking day." I was still inside her and I had no intention of moving yet.

"That was so good Conor. I've never… um, never… came like that before." She looked almost shy and nervous as she panted the words out.

"Angel, that's because you'd only ever done it with a high school boy. Now you know what it's like to be with a man." A man who would want to worship your body all day and all night if he could. *A man who would make you rethink your choice to be naked with him right now if you knew everything about him.*

"Ready for more?" I asked as I flipped her on to all fours.

"Hell yes!"

I pushed her round ass up towards my face, her soft pussy glistening towards me, her scent driving me wild with desire. My hand played with her hair and slowly pushed her head into the pillows below her.

I wanted to test her a little. "Put your hands behind your back, Ava."

She complied.

Fuck.

I held her tiny wrists together with one hand as I opened the folds of her pussy with the other, rubbing her clit once again and spreading her succulent juices across her cunt and up to that little tight rosebud, pushing a little harder against it each time. She let me. She didn't even flinch.

"You okay pet?"

"Talk Ava… how does that feel?" I asked, pushing a little harder this time and gently pressing against her tight hole. I paused with my forefinger on it, slightly testing her.

She groaned. She fucking groaned.

Aye Ava... you're too much.

My cock was about to explode. I couldn't wait any longer. I rammed into her wet pussy hard, surprising her, still holding her wrists behind her back. This time she couldn't do anything but hold still and let me set the pace. I rammed her harder than the first time until I could feel that burning and twisting up inside my balls. She screamed and moaned with desire as I quickened my pace even more. Her pussy contracted tightly around my cock and it sent us both free falling into the abyss together.

My hand released her wrists and we collapsed as I cradled her in my arms, my dick still inside her. We were one. My hands rested on her heart beating so fast. And so was mine.

Fucking beautiful.

I closed my eyes and breathed in the scent of her hair. *Another rule had been broken, and it had been the best one so far.*

CASSIDY LONDON

Chapter 15

Dublin, Ireland

Ava Jackson

Oh… My… God. It was like being deflowered for the first time all over again. Forget whatever that was back in high school. What I had just experienced at the mercy of Conor Murphy would stay with me forever. Sated, filled, and deliciously sore. I'd never felt better in all my life.

"Conor…" I murmured as I traced the length of his arm with my fingers.

He slowly opened one eye and looked at me. "I want you to drive me to the bus." I told him, still cradled in his strong arms.

"What about your father Ava? He's expecting you to do what he said." He cautioned.

"I know I fucked up, but I won't let him ruin this vacation for me. Besides, he does that. He flies off the handle easily and ends up softening up later on. It'll be fine." I assured Conor.

It wasn't fine. I knew my dad would kill me for this decision, but the reality was… I wanted more time. No. I *needed* more time with Conor. I wasn't ready for this to be a one-of-a-kind experience. Not that I was stupid. I didn't think he'd fall in love and make babies with me. This situation was wrong in every way and besides, Conor Murphy was not that kind of guy. What had happened between us had been incredible, but I wasn't naïve enough to think it could be more than that. But still... I wanted more time.

"Ava..." His deep, raspy voice filled with concern. "I don't know if this is a good decision. Pretty sure your dad will chop my balls for this, given the chance."

"I'm an adult, Conor. Either you help me, or I'll go out and find the bus by myself." I held back the smile that threatened to cross my face as I threw the blankets off and walked naked into the bathroom. I could feel his eyes boring into my naked ass and I purposefully swung my hips as I walked.

Within seconds he was behind me, his rough hands caressing my naked body and sending shivers up my spine. "Fine, you crazy girl. I'll help you. But only because I think travelling around a foreign country with no money or I.D is a terrible choice."

Gotcha Conor Murphy.

"Just understand one thing, okay?" His voice became stronger and suddenly his eyes seemed to lose that playful sparkle. "Let me make something clear to you. This thing between us... it's not anything more than just this. I will help you find that bus, but when I do, I will put you on it and that will be the end for us. Understood?"

My head nodded as I chewed my lip. *I know… I know…*

We showered and dressed more quickly than I would have liked, but we needed to get on the road and catch up to the bus. I knew the plan was to get to Belfast and spend a few days there, so I was confident we would make it before they moved on.

Thoughts of my dad kept gnawing at my mind, though. He was still reeling from my mother's betrayal ten years ago. They had quite the love affair back in the day, but she had been so much younger, and eventually their age difference had caught up to them. My mom's need to experience the world eventually caught up to her and to their relationship. She felt bored and stifled at being a wife and a mother "before her time". My parents had a quick and passionate love affair and before my mom knew what had happened, it tied her to the suburbs and had her pushing a stroller.

After she left for good, it had broken my dad. Years of therapy ensued, but despite it all, the betrayal had left permanent marks on him. He drilled it into my head that the most successful relationships are the ones when both people had a lot in common. To him that was everything; same ages, same background, same culture. Love itself wasn't enough anymore.

That's why a summer fling with a much older man in a foreign country was more than enough to have him angry with me. Let alone after what I had just told him. I loved my dad, but his issues often got in my way. Which was why it was better for him not to know everything... not yet, anyway.

But what if it's more than just a summer fling, Ava?

I pushed those thoughts to the back of my head.

"All right, so you said the next stop is Belfast?" He asked. "That's only about two hours from here, so let's get on the road now and maybe this can all be resolved by the afternoon." Conor muttered.

"We must go the jump site to get my truck, though. Can't drive you two hours on the back of my bike, can I?"

"Whatever you say Conor." I giggled. He looked away. Conor was getting more distant by the minute. Even trying to lighten the mood with a little flirting wasn't having the same effect.

We walked outside and around the back to where he kept his bike. Conor passed me a helmet and showed me how to sit on the bike. "Having all that roaring metal between my legs is kind of exciting." I teased. I hiked my miniskirt all the way up exposing my panties, lifted my leg, and swung it over. "Is this ok?" My pussy was directly on his leather seat, no shame.

"Is that all that does it for you, princess?" He mocked. "Because I know otherwise."

Finally, a reaction.

He sat in front of me and grabbed my arms, wrapping them around his body. Holding him close, my body pressed to his while we rode, was exhilarating.

***

I saw the jump site sign come into focus and felt my heart leap a little. Conor parked the bike outside the front office entrance and jumped off. "Stay here a minute. I have to run inside a moment."

Staying put was not my forte. I needed to explore. Walking around the empty jump site made me reminisce about how quickly everything had changed. I had arrived in Ireland for a vacation with my girlfriends and was now about to take a road trip with a man that made me question everything I thought I knew…

One guy walked by and did a double take. I smiled back, recognizing him as the instructor who had jumped with Sam. He answered with a wink and my gaze followed him into the building. As the door opened, I heard Conor's voice barking out, "Patrick!" If there was ever a warning, that was it.

Next thing I knew, he was calling me in too. "Ava!" I

practically ran through the door. Conor stood next to me immediately, one hand moving to my lower back and the other on my shoulder protectively.

"Boys, I need to leave for a day. Ava here missed her tour bus and I'm driving her to Belfast to reconnect with it."

Someone snickered in the back. "My arse you are."

Conor's eyes narrowed and a low grumbling sound emerged from him. "Sorry boss." Came the quick response.

"Finn will be in charge until I'm back. Don't fuck up, boys." Those were his last words before he grabbed my hand and pulled me out the door. I waved and smiled at them as I was being dragged out. "Bye boys", I called back to them. Then I heard a bunch of chatter and a couple of whistles and smiled to myself.

"Why are you aggressive with so them?" I questioned as soon as we were out of earshot.

"Not your business, Ava." Conor growled back at me.

Shit. This guy definitely had issues.

Chapter 16

Dublin, Ireland

Conor Murphy

Feelings of dread came over me as we approached my red pickup truck. Opening the cab door, I motioned for her to get in. After driving for about twenty minutes in silence, she spoke again.

"Why were you so aggressive with them?" She questioned me. *Again.* "A morning like we had should have put you in a good mood…" She pressed on, fluttering her damn lashes at me, making me laugh. *Such a tease.*

"Fine, okay. I didn't like the way they looked at you. It was just like when you came to jump that first day. Every man in the place was undressing you in his mind. Imagining himself pawing at your body."

I felt my knuckles grip the steering wheel.

"Not everyone has honorable intentions, Ava. My guys are good men, but they think with their dicks." I was feeling more and more protective of her by the minute and it was stressing me the fuck out.

"So… kind of the way you did earlier this morning?" She giggled. "Give me a little credit, Conor. I know you

145

rescued me last night, but I'm not as innocent and incapable of handling things as you might think."

"Anyway… enough about me. I want to know about you."

Fuck… where was she going with this?

"There's nothing interesting to tell." I answered gruffly.

"Hmm… somehow, I think there's quite a lot." She began. "Let's start with an easy question. How did you get into skydiving?"

Shit. She had me at skydiving. Talking about the skies was something I couldn't say no to. "It's the freefall that keeps me coming back." I whispered. "Without it, I can't function. The world becomes too heavy. Skydiving helps me stay sober, Ava. When I'm freefalling, everything is perfect."

"Yeah…" She said wistfully, my comment about staying sober barely seeming to register. "I hadn't expected that. I thought I would feel the earth's gravity pulling me down, but it wasn't like that at all. I felt like I was floating, flying even." Turning my head to her, I saw the glow in her eyes. They sparkled, and I felt it opening me up.

"Conor… I know the guys at the site introduced you as ex-military but… did your substance abuse happen because of your experiences at war?"

Not. Going. There.

I turned my head away from her and kept my eyes on the road. She was pushing me too hard. She already had too much on me. I needed to pull my shit together and remind her this was only lasting another few hours.

She retreated a little when I didn't answer and an uncomfortable silence blanketed the surrounding air. The green pastures of the countryside flew by as we drove in silence.

Minutes seem to drag on.

Then suddenly. "Look! Sheep!" She cooed. "They're so cute!"

I looked over at her, her face sparkling with wonder at the tiny, fluffy white balls that seemed to float past the windows. "Sheep?" I questioned. "Really? Don't they have those in America?"

"Hilarious!" Ava giggled, slapping my bicep. It was such a natural thing to do amongst friends or lovers, but the second her hand connected with my arm, I swear a jolt of electricity hit us both.

"Conor!" She screamed. "Watch out!" Snapping my focus back on the road, I swerved and had a near miss with the car in front of me. Slamming on my breaks, it flung us both front and back swiftly. Instinctively, my arm came out across her body to hold her still. Her expression mirrored my own. Shock and apprehension at what could have been.

I felt frozen in time. Everything that had happened since I first saw Ava Jackson in the airport had been surreal. And my carelessness had nearly thrown it away.

We stopped in our tracks and found ourselves in what looked like a major traffic jam.

Ava was shaking and gripping the sides of the door fiercely.

"Babe, you all right?" My hand turned her chin, to see her better.

"Uh… I think so." She mumbled, her eyes filling with tears. "I got scared."

"I'm so sorry pet. I got distracted, I don't know what came over me."

"It's okay. No worries, we're all right and no one got hurt." She said, putting on a brave face and shaking it off.

The near accident hadn't changed the air of electricity between us though.

In fact, it may have even enhanced it. I watched as her beautiful breasts raised and lowered with each breath. Her pert little nipples I had tasted just hours ago poked shamelessly through her clothing. Pink blotches of stress peppered her skin as her complexion turned a shade of red more vibrant than her hair.

She was fucking excited. I could sense it. *I could fucking smell it.* The adrenaline had turned her on, and I had to taste it.

"You're right babe. But this jam will delay us. What time is the bus supposed to leave Belfast?" I said, trying to shake off the need to pull over at the side of the road and fuck her senseless.

"Uh... I... I think..." She went on flustered and unable to get her words out. Finally, after a long deep breath that held me hostage, she spoke. "This looks like it will be quite the delay... how do you propose we pass the time?" Her eyes fluttered beneath her lashes as her hand walked its way across my thigh toward the visible bulge in my jeans. She raked her nails over my cock like she had done it a million times before.

CASSIDY LONDON

Chapter 17

Dublin, Ireland

Ava Jackson

I knew he was dangerous the first moment I met him, and truth be told, I still knew little about him. But what I knew made me want to rip my clothes off every time he looked at me. His eyes seemed to eat me up as he dragged his gaze lasciviously across my body. I could feel my body responding to just a flicker of those emerald eyes.

Just the sight of him made me blush and my mind bring forth memories of his face between my legs and the tickling of his beard on my most sensitive parts.

He was everything I shouldn't get involved with. Sixteen years my senior and foreign, with a sketchy past he seemed to want to avoid discussing. However, all that was overshadowed by the burning desire in his eyes whenever he looked at me. I swear this man could really see me. His eyes burned with intensity unlike anyone I'd ever met. With every look, I wanted to give him more of myself. Share with him more of my mind, body, and soul. One look from him and my body responded immediately. I felt myself craving his physical touch as much as his deep gaze into my soul and his words in my mind.

Just like the freefall, there was no choice but to give in. It was instant and surreal and there was no choice but to surrender to it.

Our moments together were limited, but I would not waste a second. I would make the most of every single moment.

"Ava Jackson, you naughty little girl... I should like to spank you for such dirty suggestions." His voice rumbled through the car with a sexy tone to it.

His raspy Irish accent was enough to get me off, but his words... oh, his words. I loved the way he told me exactly what he wanted to do. I had never known what words like that could do. And it seemed I'd been waiting my whole life to hear them.

Conor Murphy made me feel bold and confident in a way I never had. Being with him made words come out of my mouth I never even knew existed in my head.

"Conor..." I whispered as my hand crept up his thigh towards the bulging mass in his jeans. Those green eyes stared through me with fire as he allowed me to open his belt buckle. I watched as his eyes darted from me to the windows of the truck and neighboring cars. He released his seatbelt and slid back in his seat, opening his legs wider. Clear suggestion.

The corners of his mouth smirked a little, giving way to encouraging my actions. His arm became heavier on my back, pushing my face lower towards his crotch. I now lay flat across the front of the seat with my ass in the air as I slid my hand inside his pants and freed his hard cock. A loud but controlled growl rumbled through the truck.

"Avaaaa…" He moaned now, breathing heavier, his hand fisting my hair as I licked him root to tip before sliding him into my mouth. He was so huge, I could feel him tickling the back of my throat.

He had pulled my hair gently, but he yanked it harder as he pushed my head lower into his crotch. I gagged a little and he released me, immediately moving his hand lower down my body and sliding it under my skirt. Then something landed on top of my ass, covering it, seconds before his hand slipped under my skirt and pushing it up to my waist. He squeezed my ass hard as I continued to suck him.

"Fuck, you're killing me Ava…" I smiled inwardly. He groaned again as I felt his fingers slide between my legs and cup my dripping pussy.

I moaned as he pushed up against my slit, still super sensitive from this morning's adventure. After not being touched by a man in so long, to have these sensations twice in a matter of hours was incredible. "So wet babe… y'er so fucking wet. I love it." He murmured as his fingers slid in and out of my pussy. I heard the wet sounds of his fingers working it, and I increased my pace sucking him to match his strokes.

"Hang on, baby." He said, releasing my hair. "Need to move the car. Traffic letting up." He said between labored breaths.

Conor's hand gripped the steering wheel while his fingers stayed inside me with his other hand. He was holding me still, from the inside, preventing me from rolling forward off the seat.

Hollowing out my cheeks further, I continued to suck him harder and faster as the car inched slowly forward. Conor groaned louder. "You're killing me, lass." He moaned. The car stopped and his hand went back to pulling at my hair. He pulled it so hard that my head raised up, sucking his cock as I went. My tongue lapped up the drips of glistening pre-come that had formed on the head.

"Angel?" He whispered. "You alright?" I smiled only for a brief second before he pushed me down again, this time setting the pace himself and literally fucking my mouth with his dick. His hips pushed up and down, and he controlled my head, pushing it down and pulling me back up again by my hair. He was pumping his cock faster and faster. It hurt, but it felt even better to know I could please him. He wanted it so badly.

"Yess… almost there, pet. Keep going…" He groaned as the car pushed forward a little more. I could feel his dick pulsing and I knew he was close. I kept at it, harder and deeper until tears stung my eyes. His whole body shuddered as his dick pumped and his hot salty seed flooded my mouth. I squeezed his balls, swallowing every last drop as I went. I hollowed out my cheeks and pulled off of him.

He was holding the wheel white knuckled, sweat glistening on the side of his neck. I pushed up and off my elbows as he closed his zipper.

"So good babe…" He murmured. "You okay, though? I didn't mean to be that rough about it. You sucked me so good."

"Not at all… I'm fine." I said as he watched me wipe the corners of my eyes.

He grinned. "Good…'cause that was barely a preview of how rough I like it. And don't think this is over, Ava." He continued. "Mark my words. I will have you riding my cock one more time before I have to put you on that bus."

I giggled nervously but could feel my body come alive by his words. I felt myself dripping in my panties from his unfinished business with me. Silence filled the cabin as I stared at him. He was so gorgeous. I don't even think he knew how much he affected me; how he affected everyone.

***

Looking out the window at the traffic, I wondered if we would make it on time. We were driving again, but still at a ridiculously slow speed. Conor's hand rested on my bare thigh, dangerously close to my throbbing privates. His fingers wrapped around the inside of my leg possessively. His pinky slid on the edge of my lace panties, slipping in and caressing that inner crease. He then tapped his pinkie over my pussy covered by my panties, which enhanced the sensations. Instinctively, I spread my thighs open and hiked my skirt up further, giving a little moan. I lowered the neckline of the shirt he had lent me so he could see my swelled breasts, which I wanted him to fondle so badly. I wished we could stay like this for longer. My chest tightened at the thought of leaving him forever in just a few hours and I immediately pushed those thoughts back into the crevices of my mind.

There were still some things that Conor didn't know. Yes, I hadn't been with anyone in college, but there had been more than just unrequited love that caused it. The boy from high school had been my first love, my childhood best friend turned boyfriend, lost my virginity on prom night kind of love.

Despite my dad's warnings that it was too soon, we had planned to marry after college. Dreams of babies and white picket fences was all we talked about. Then, during the first year of college, second term to be exact, it happened. I got the call in my dorm room in the middle of the night; a drunk driver had hit his car. That night, my heart broke into a million little pieces. In an instant, I lost my love and the entire life I had envisioned for us.

Then, more heartache. At his funeral, I was hit with the surprise of a lifetime. I remember a guy standing a little further back, crying his eyes out. He wasn't like the other friends that had come. He was dressed in goth attire, with lime green hair and black eyeliner streaming down his face. He caught my attention because he looked so sad. I felt for him, but I also couldn't understand why he was there. Had he known Ryan? Ryan was a clean-cut, preppy guy. None of his friends dressed like that. And I knew everyone in Ryan's life. After the service, I approached the boy. I remember putting my hand on his shoulder and asked, "How did you know Ryan?"

He looked up from his hands, his face running with eyeliner, and uttered the words that shattered the remnants of my mangled heart. "I loved him, Ava. I know you did too, but there was also a lot you didn't know about Ryan."

His words shot me clean through.

"He would have told you, Ava... he wanted you to know about us. He didn't want to hurt you though."

A familiar lump in my throat appeared as I

remembered.

Losing love seemed to be a common theme in my life. My mother had left my father and I in search of herself. My first boyfriend, the love of my life, had died and left me to find out he had been having an affair with a man the whole time. Then, just as I regained confidence and felt ready to move on, the T.A that I had fallen for used me and cheated on me.

To say I felt unlucky in love was an understatement. Love was an ideal, a dream even, but never something that panned out long term. It was better to keep my feelings under wraps and safe inside the confines of my heart where they couldn't be trampled on.

My feelings for Conor were growing by the minute, but something was nagging at my mind. He had clammed up earlier when I pressed him for information. I knew a foreign affair with an older man whose life seemed worlds away from my own was definitely a situation to walk away from. But even so, I wanted to know more. I was looking for a reason, a bigger reason, it wouldn't work. Something I could use to prove to my heart he was no good for me. He had gone back to steady driving with both hands now on the steering wheel, and my mind could focus more.

"Conor… can I ask you something?" I ventured.

"I'd rather slide my hand between your legs again and

watch you come in the front seat of my truck, pet." He grumbled, his voice still thick with desire despite his recent orgasm.

"Not that I don't want that…" I giggled, gently pushing his pawing hands down, "but I want to know a little more about you."

His eyes glazed over as his hand moved away. "One question pet, but I make no promises I will answer."

CASSIDY LONDON

Chapter 18

Belfast, Northern Ireland

Conor Murphy

She was pushing for more again. She was curious and had asked a few too many questions already. I had been careful, though. So, I stuck to the basics. She already knew I had been a para-trooper in Afghanistan, so I continued with that and confirmed how the four back-to-back missions had taken their toll on me. I continued talking as she held my hand and listened. She didn't ask for more, but just accepted what I gave her, squeezing my hand in solidarity as I spoke.

"After they discharged me and I came back to Ireland, I struggled to find a place for myself. Demons of my youth called, and it wasn't long before I turned to drugs to numb the pain."

I took another deep breath. "What I didn't tell you before Ava, was that the world of drugs was a world I knew well from my adolescence. It's been a problem of mine for a long time now."

"It wasn't until a friend of mine, Eoghan actually– from the pub? Not sure you can remember in the state you were…" I looked to her, but she shook her head. "Anyway, he reminded me about the thrill of the jump and convinced me to hold off on my next hit until I jumped with him. He saved my life. For the second time."

"We started skydiving regularly, and eventually I became clean enough to get a job and, as you know now, own my place."

"Do you remember what I said about the freefall?" I asked wistfully, feeling it in my bones as I spoke. "Yes..." She whispered smiling, her warmth flooding the depths of my soul.

I smiled at her reaction. "Exactly. That's the moment. The moment that trumps the high of any manufactured drug. I can't live without it now. I became one with the jump site. Like I said before... some days it's the only thing that keeps me alive."

"I'm glad that Eoghan was there to help you and how far you've come, Conor. You should be proud of yourself." I nodded. She was sweet.

"I want to ask you again though... what prompted the drugs in the first place?"

Fuck. I said too much. I should have known better.

"Ava... what I've told you is more than I've ever told anyone. But don't push me for more. It's enough!" I yelled unintentionally. She was getting too close. I couldn't risk it. She didn't need that kind of baggage,

162

not to mention the fear. The last thing I wanted was for her to be scared of me.

She looked taken aback. Confusion crossed her beautiful face, making me feel like shit.

***

As we crossed into Northern Ireland, I felt an uneasiness come over me. I could feel it in my bones, exactly the same way I could feel her coursing through my veins. I knew it was wrong, but I didn't care. I needed her. I didn't know why, only that I did. She captivated me, made me come alive after what felt like a long and dark slumber.

We tracked down the hotel in Belfast and soon pulled in to the car park. We held hands but were both quiet, knowing it was almost over.

The girl at the front desk immediately fluttered her eyelashes as I made eye contact. I was used to that. Happened fucking everywhere. When I was younger, it made me one hell of a cocky bastard, but as I got older, I knew that shit didn't last. Girls, especially younger women, were all about what they thought you were or what they wanted you to be. Then, when they heard the bad and the ugly, they were gone. Better that way though…

"Hi there, we're looking for the Eurotour bus?" I asked as I wrapped my arm around Ava protectively. I watched as the desk girl's reaction changed upon seeing Ava. Her eyes darted from mine to Ava's and back again. Surprise and then jealousy and definite judgement crossed her face.

"Um… yes, they're still here, leaving in the morning I believe."

Ava snuggled into me and looked up into my eyes.

"The morning?" I repeated. *Fuck… I had more time.*

"I'd like to call my friend's room." Ava said to the girl. "Samantha Campbell and Adriana Acosta." She continued, her fingers fidgeting nervously on the desk.

The desk girl motioned for Ava to come around the side to use the house phone. She put the phone to her and I made an impulse decision. Slipping the desk girl my credit card, I booked a room for the night. I would take advantage of whatever time I had left with this beautiful girl, even if every moment spent together made it harder to say goodbye. She would not leave Ireland before I fucked her well and good one more time.

The desk clerk's voice brought me back to earth. "Ahem… Sir— Mr. Conor, here is your room pass." She slipped me the pass and stared in Ava's direction with distaste. Fucking women. They could never be happy for someone else? They always had to play this jealous bitch card.

Ava walked back towards me looking down. "They didn't answer, but I guess they're off on an excursion. They should be back soon. Glad we made it here in time…" she trailed off, looking down at her feet.

She was about to say goodbye.

"So, I guess… I guess this is it, huh?" She said, finally looking up.

I stepped closer, breathing in her delicious scent. My hand ran across her cheek and up into her hair. I watched as her breath hitched at my touch. She chewed on that luscious lower lip, her desire hitting me straight in the chest and in the pants.

"C'mon pet, I'll stay till they come back, okay? Let's go wait at the bar."

"Conor! Thank you!" She squealed, throwing her arms around my waist and hugging me. I nearly laughed. She looked like a child with her head buried in my chest like that. Damn, I wanted to pick her up and claim that pouty little mouth of hers. Thoughts of bending her over that hotel desk and fucking her senseless until she screamed my name clouded my vision.

Hold tight, Conor…

"Besides, you need to call your father and tell him you're back on the bus." I said, tapping her button nose

Ava took my hand as we walked towards the bar.

"You're right. And Conor...? Thanks for getting me here and for waiting." She continued as we slid into the bar stools.

"Babe, did you really think I would leave you at the door and drive off?" I asked.

She giggled. Giggled that sweet innocent Ava laugh that made my heart ache. *I am a grown man. What was happening to me?*

Chapter 19

Belfast, Northern Ireland

Ava Jackson

Conor's hand was on my bare thigh, his thumb absently caressing my skin. We'd been sitting there about an hour, trying to keep the conversation light. He had been asking me questions about my life and I had told him about my mom. His eyes had softened when I spoke about her. It was a painful subject for me and although I couldn't tell exactly what he was thinking, his presence and empathy was comforting at least.

Talking had kept the sexual tension down a notch at least. Not completely gone, just slightly hovering beneath the surface. The touch of his hand on my skin was giving me shivers. I felt flushed but wasn't sure if it was because of him or the drinks.

I was on my second drink when I heard my name being screamed across the bar. Suddenly, I was conscious of still wearing my clothes from the night before but now with a man's… *this man's*, oversize shirt on top.

"Where the FUCK have you been, Ava Jackson!" Screamed Adriana as she flung her arms around me. "Girl, we were freaking the fuck out!" continued Sam.

"We asked Mike to wait for you or to go back or something, but he wouldn't! Insisted it was company policy to keep going, said it was in our waiver form and everything!"

Adriana was running at full speed, her words flying out of her mouth faster than I could absorb them. "Honestly Ava, I wanted to call your dad, but Sam said it would only make shit worse for you. Besides, Mike said he was sure you'd make it to the next stop. Apparently, this happens at least once every summer and people just figure it out."

Sam's mouth fell open, and she stayed like that for a minute before she spoke. "Jesus Christ, you're here with the skydiving guy!"

"Had you girls been worried, then perhaps you should have called the police?" Conor's voice boomed. "What kind of friends are you exactly? How long did it take you to notice that Ava wasn't with you anymore?"

Well… this didn't sound like it was going well.

"His name's Conor." I said, sliding off the bar stool and holding his arm. Conor's arm quickly wrapped around my waist protectively.

"Oh… My… God." Sam mouthed as she took a step back behind Adriana, who was still staring down Conor. "Did you fuck him?" She continued, pointing to Conor. Despite her efforts, discreet she wasn't.

"How is that any of your business?" Conor spit out. "If not for me, your friend could have been half-dead on the floor of the pub toilet last night."

This was getting a little too heated for my liking.

Adri and Sam's eyes darted back and forth between Conor and I, then to each other. I had to intervene. "It's fine girls, nothing terrible happened. Conor found me and intervened before anything bad happened."

"Really?" Adri questioned.

"Yes, really." I assured her.

My friends looked shell-shocked. "Wow… Thanks for taking care of Ava."

"We looked for you Ava, but then that fight broke out and Mike kept screaming for everyone to get on the bus. It was only when the bus was on the highway that we realized you weren't there."

Sam cried. "Ava, I'm so sorry! We were all so drunk and just not thinking about each other."

My friends were a mess. We hugged and cried as I continued to assure them it was okay. "Where did you stay last night Ava? Did you go back to the motel?" Adri asked.

Conor had sat back down on the bar stool while we had been talking. Just then, he reached over and pulled me in between his legs, his arms crossed at my hips.

"Uh…" I began.

"With me. She stayed with me." Conor answered for me. "But for the record, I don't fuck drunk girls I find in bars." He said gruffly.

My friends just stared.

"So you take them home and watch them sleep from the couch then?" Adri challenged him. I felt his hands tighten on my hip.

"How gentlemanly of you… Conor was it?" She continued.

Conor stood up, practically raising me off my feet as he placed me down next to him. He moved me like I was a doll, making me feel small and so hot for him all at the same time.

I watched as he stared Adriana down, his six-foot-two frame and green eyes burning into her. "That attitude will get you into trouble, you know…" She didn't respond. Conor could be very menacing when he wanted to be.

Turning, he said my name. "Ava." His tone was nothing short of a command. I stood up. This was it. He was leaving. My chest tightened up as I blinked furiously, trying to hold back the tears that threatened to expose my feelings. How could this have happened?

Barely twenty-four hours with this man and I felt like I was about to lose something I'd never be able to find again.

"I'm expecting you in exactly one hour, Ava. Not a minute more. Don't make me come looking for you." His eyes twinkled as he slid a room key into the pocket of his own shirt that still covered my body.

Then, he turned and walked out of the bar as we all stared at those tight, low-slung jeans that covered his exceptionally tight ass.

My heart fluttered at the same time my panties warmed.

I could be bad for one more night...

CASSIDY LONDON

Chapter 20

Belfast, Northern Ireland

Conor Murphy

I could feel their eyes on me as I walked out. Fuck them all. I knew they were judging me, thinking I had taken advantage of Ava's situation, but I didn't care. I knew better and so did Ava. All I cared about was getting more time with her. I'd seen an opportunity, and I had taken it.

Besides, tonight would be the last time. If she came. I made myself laugh. Who the fuck was I kidding, she'd come. I would make her come six ways till Sunday. Ava Jackson would never forget the name Conor Murphy. A low growl arose in my throat as I adjusted the throbbing mass in my crotch. I'd had no choice but to walk out of that bar. With Ava between my legs, and the heated conversation with her friends, I was ready to either punch the wall or rip all her clothes off and take her right there. Possibly both.

I had one hour.

I needed to clear my mind before she arrived. A shower would do it. I could always think in the shower. I ripped my clothes off, hastily throwing them on the bed as I walked towards the shower. The hot water was soothing at first. It calmed my nerves. But soon things changed. The lush curves of her body and the sounds she'd made when I was balls deep inside her this morning found their way back to the front of my mind, and made my dick throb ever so painfully.

Should have taken a fucking cold shower.

It seemed like I'd had a permanent hard-on since I met this woman. How life would go back to normal after she left was beyond me right now. The ride had been both brutal and incredible. Still, I didn't believe she'd suck me off in traffic, let alone how she'd gotten me to open about my life. There was so much more to this girl. The more time I spent with her, the more I learned and the more I wanted to know. I sighed. Who was I kidding? That kind of happiness wasn't for me. That wasn't my story. Mine was darker and more sinister than that. And if Ava knew the truth about me, she'd never come to my room tonight or any other night.

Tonight, would have to be the last time.

Maybe leaving this girl with good memories of me would somehow save a small part of my soul. My heart was ripping at the thought of it now.

I closed my eyes, threw my head back, and let the water run down my body. It helped to calm me, somewhat.

My muscles felt tight and achy from sitting in the truck during the long ride to Belfast. I needed to move to release this pent-up energy that was simmering just below the surface. Not that I was complaining, but getting a blowjob in the confined space of my truck is never an easy thing when you're six-foot-two.

Wrapping a towel around myself, I grabbed the phone to order room service. We hadn't eaten in a few hours and I was famished. I figured food was going to be a priority for her, too. The whiskey at the bar had coated my stomach for a short time, but now I needed something more substantial.

After ordering an array of pretty much everything on the menu, I sat down on the couch and opened my email. A quick check-in with the boys at the jump site was on the agenda. I had to make sure the day had gone well. Having not missed a day of work in two years, not being there today had been a big deal for me. Wouldn't have had it any other way, though. My day with Ava had been incredible… and it wasn't over yet.

Arthur had done his duty and emailed the reports of the day. I was going through them when I heard a knock at the door. "Just a bloody minute." I grumbled, annoyed at being interrupted. At least room service was quick.

I opened the door in my towel, my hair dripping all over me, fully expecting the room service guy. Instead, I was greeted by Ava wearing tiny little shorts and t-shirt. Her hair was soaking wet and the water dripping down her shirt made her braless chest look like she was at a wet t-shirt contest. Typically, I would have appreciated a look like that on an attractive woman. But seeing Ava like this in the hallway sent waves of anger running through me.

"Get your arse in here!" I barked at her. "What the hell are you doing roaming the halls dressed like that? Besides, you're early."

"Ooh… sorry... had you not yet finished with your previous fuck? Should I come back?" She teased.

An uncontrollable growl filled the room. "Jesus, woman!" Grabbing her by the back of her neck, my mouth crashed down on to hers with an urgency greater than I had even realized. She felt so good under my touch. I loved how her words were spicy and teasing, but her body was soft and easily molded to my touch.

My hands slipped under her wet t-shirt, cupping her breasts and running my thumbs over her hardened nipples. She moaned my name as I flicked and rolled them beneath my fingers, my mouth leaving a trail of gentle bite marks down her neck.

"Conor please…." she moaned.

"Please what my darling?" It was my turn to tease now. "You just got here. I'm not giving you what you want just yet. Besides, we need to eat first."

She groaned a response.

"And I'm surprised Adriana allowed you to come see me. I don't think she likes me much." I said, chuckling and knowing full well that nothing would have stopped my girl from coming tonight. I slipped my hands out of her shirt and pinched her nipples to harden them further as they stared at me through her wet shirt. *FUCK.*

"Well, she thinks I'm crazy and you're right, she's not the biggest fan of yours, but I told her to back off. It's just one night, right?" She shrugged her delicate little shoulders and flicked her hair away.

Yeah. Just one more night. My heart sank.

"Did you call your dad?" I asked, eager to change the subject.

"Yeah…" A look of sadness came over her beautiful face. "I did. I told him I used the money he wired me to catch a train to Belfast and find the group again. He was super pissed that I wasn't coming home, but I made Sam talk to him and assure him I was here and I was safe."

I smiled. Ava had a way of getting what she wanted. I really liked that about her. It wasn't immature; it was something quite the opposite actually.

"The bus leaves at eight tomorrow morning. I must get

back to the girls' room to shower and get dressed before that though." She trailed off.

I had stopped listening. Details, just details. The sound of knocking at the door interrupted us. "Room service." I winked. A waiter stood with a procession of carts outside the door, and I saw there were four more waiters just like him standing in the hallway. I noticed passersby's stopping to look at what was going on. They probably thought it was someone important staying here.

I watched as they rolled the carts inside, and Ava stood wide-eyed at all the food platters. I tipped them and they graciously thanked me and left.

"I wasn't sure what you liked, so I ordered a little bit of everything, pet." I said, uncovering the platters of salads, grilled lemon chicken and pasta dishes, desserts, and mixed platters that had so many colorful mini bites it was like being at a buffet.

"That's a shit ton of food, babe!" She said as she picked cucumbers from the salad and crunched down on them.

"Ooh…" her eyes widened even bigger as she lifted the top off the fruit and chocolate fondue platter. "Fancy!"

I motioned to her empty glass. "Wine?"

"Always." She smiled up at me.

"Fuel up little one. You'll need the energy for what I have planned for us afterwards."

Her eyelids fluttered at my words and a slow blush crept up her entire neck. She knew… I meant business. She knew I was going to fuck her again and again.

CASSIDY LONDON

Chapter 21

Belfast, Northern Ireland

Ava Jackson

As we ate, we chatted. Conor was unusually talkative tonight. Maybe it was because our time was limited or maybe because he was finally feeling comfortable enough to let his guard down. Either way, it made me happy. He talked a lot about skydiving and the different places in the world where he'd jumped.

He told me how he had rebuilt the office and jump site all on his own. While working for the previous owner, he had been more than just an instructor, he had done every job possible on site. From manual labor to accounting, jumping tandem with first timers, to coaching experienced jumpers for competitions. Conor was even a certified rigger which most instructors were not. Being a rigger was a specialized job that required a license and a certain affinity for ropes and buckles. Riggers were the guys who packed the chutes and made sure everything was up to code. As he spoke about tying knots and securing chutes, a dark little spot in my mind conjured up images of better ways to put that talent to good use. I may not have a lot of experience, but I was creative and curious. *If only we had more time together…*

Just then, as if he was reading my mind, Conor suddenly stopped talking. "What are you thinking about, pet?"

"Nothing…" I whispered, lost inside my head, and the sadness probably showing in my response.

"Doesn't look like nothing…" He repeated, moving closer and pulling me on to his lap. His hands began to possessively explore their way up my thighs and beneath my shorts.

"Fuck Ava! No panties?"

I giggled. *I loved watching him get all riled up.*

His hands were everywhere now, taking stock of every inch of my body and making my temperature skyrocket in every place I needed attention. "I should spank that pretty ass of yours for strolling through the halls like a little tart." He growled.

"A tart?" I giggled. "What the fuck is a tart? Like a pie?"

"No, you silly American, not a fucking wholesome apple pie. Anything but. In fact…" Conor continued as he pulled me across his lap and yanked my shorts down to my knees. My ass in the air, he grabbed and squeezed my cheeks hard as he pushed his hand down my spine, forcing my head lower down. I yelped a little.

"A tart… is a naughty little whore. A good fuck." He

paused as I sucked in air. "You all right there, pet?" He whispered, stopping for a second.

I nodded. The feelings were clouding my head and I was unable to think straight. It took me a moment, but I pulled it together. Turning my head, I smirked. "Are you going to come through or are you all talk and no action… Sir?"

The sound of spanking skin on skin reverberated through the room as his open palm connected with my ass cheeks. "You think you're funny? Did you think I wasn't serious?" He demanded harshly.

Words suddenly became more difficult than ever.

"Ava?" Conor questioned.

"I'm okay…" I said slowly, my heart racing. "I think I kind of liked it…" Somewhat ashamed of how much his spanking me had turned me on, I felt my folds moisten.

Conor chuckled.

"That first one was for parading around with all your goods on display. And this one…" He spanked me again even harder this time and tears stung my eyes from the pain. "Is for being such a goddam' tease."

He turned my chin and looked deep into my eyes before leaning over and kissing my mouth gently.

I smiled through the tears that were making my eyelashes stick together.

"But this one…" Again, pain seared on my behind. "Is because I fucking love this round, plump ass of yours." He continued as his hand spanked my right cheek down again harder than all the times before.

He rubbed my ass in circles, slowing the burn as I tried to regain my breathing. My pussy was actually wet from his harsh touch. I felt him lean and get something and suddenly something cool and wet was circling my ass now. He had grabbed a piece of ice off the drinks cart. With his other hand, his fingers slipped suddenly into my very wet pussy. I wasn't sure if I was calming down or getting even more excited, but I was positive I didn't want it to stop.

"Pet, the things I want to do to you…" He slipped the ice onto my rosebud and pulsed it there. I felt my groans getting louder. Both holes were being teased. It was too much, almost more than I could bear. He whispered with his accent and hot breath right behind my ear. That raspy voice made me moan in response before he picked me up and sat me on his lap as if I weighed nothing at all. My hair whipped around us as I threw my head back and wrapped my legs around his waist, grinding into his tight jeans with my bare skin.

"You make me want to do things I've never even thought of before, babe." I answered shamelessly. My breasts bounced lightly under my wet t-shirt as I pushed them into his chest. My hips ground and rocked on his obvious hard-on beneath his bath towel.

He had left the ice cube wedged in my ass and the erotic sensation of it was overwhelming. The coolness was seeping out, coating every part of my hot flesh, making me feel sexy and wild in a way I never had before.

He smiled that crooked smile of his that I loved with a really naughty glint in his eyes. There was something different about this man. Something I had missed in anyone I'd ever met before. We had a connection. An intensely strong physical one for sure, but it was more than that, too. I felt like I'd lived many lifetimes with this man.

"Seriously, I feel so deliciously dirty with you… I don't want it to end." The lump in my throat that had been steadily growing since this morning made its appearance again. Bigger and stronger this time, and threatening to inflict even more damage.

Conor's lips crashed into mine. Brutal and harsh. A kiss that said everything that words couldn't say. We moaned into our mouths, greedily licking and sucking each other's tongues like we could not get enough of one another. He lifted my t-shirt up over my head and threw it across the room as he kissed me with such fierce passion, I felt I was going to burst with come, and I had not even been penetrated yet. I sat naked and ready on his lap, my arms entwined around his neck, and sucking his mouth while his busy hands played with my ass and teased my clit.

His strong arms lifted me off and placed my feet back on the ground. "Don't move an inch pet." He commanded as he dropped his bath towel to the floor. Watching Conor undress did things to my body that were indescribable. My brain seemed to turn to mush at the sight of his bare chest and body. I touched myself and grabbed my breast in the other hand, as he was now naked before me, each muscle glistening in the light. He stood before me waiting for a moment, allowing me to take in the sight of him. His cock sprung out to attention, enticing me as he grabbed his shaft and fisted himself from root to tip.

"Come, baby…" he called. I stepped forward only twice before he grabbed me in his arms and threw me up against the wall. "I've been wanting to bury myself inside you ever since your hot little mouth left my dick this afternoon." He whispered in my ear.

With Conor's hands wrapped around my hips and my back supported by the wall, he easily rubbed his naked cock against my swollen wet pussy lips, teasing me and preparing me. "Y'er so fucking wet for me, pet. God, how I wish I could fuck you bare." My eyes flew open in shock and stared at him. Not that I would be totally unprotected, I was on the Pill out of habit… but still.

My heart said yes but brain told me NO. Conor smiled as he brushed the back of his hand across my cheek. "Don't worry my sweet. What I'd like to do and what I know is right are two different things. I'd also like to tie you up in a jump harness and suspend you from my goddamn ceiling like a beautiful fucking chandelier… but again… not on the menu for tonight." He breathed into my neck.

My breath hitched with shock at his words, but there was no time to think about it. His fingers had found their way inside my body and were working their magic, tweaking and circling, beckoning my orgasm towards him as I moaned and cursed and screamed his name.

Within minutes, I felt that familiar warm tingling curl up inside me and reverberate through my body from the inside out. Conor held me tight against the wall, his strong arms holding me tight as I shuddered into his arms and screamed.

"I need to taste you now." The urgency in his voice was clear. Conor laid me on the bed as I continued to squirm and my toes curled. Spreading my legs wide and dipping his head down, his hair and beard tickled inside my thighs. He inhaled and whispered "So sweet." He winked at me before opening my wet swollen folds with his fingers to slowly kiss and suck on my clit and folds. He was going to kill me slowly for sure. So this is what being fucked was really like. What the fuck was

I doing before this?

"I can't, not again. Conor please!" I wailed. "It's too sensitive!" I moaned louder and squirmed even more beneath him and I felt his strong hands gipping me and holding me down.

"You will come for me again, Ava. I love watching you lose control like that. You're so beautiful when you let yourself give in to the pleasure. Don't think, just feel baby."

His words, combined with that expert tongue, helped me to relax and let it all go. Conor started with a slow gentle sucking, then switched to licking and lapping up and down, followed by a circular motion I thought would drive me over the edge. He continued that way steadily until it felt like I was going to explode again. He took me to that edge of a mind-blowing orgasm and then backed off. He slowed down only to speed back up again. He teased me like this so many times I lost count of how many times I had come. I had no choice but to give in to the feeling, letting it carry me over the edge into bliss. I shuddered, feeling the release deep within me, and a rush of fluids released from my body. It was exhilarating and terrifying and so intimate all at the same time. I was getting wilder and more savage with each orgasm. Conor didn't move. He lay there lapping up my juices like it was nectar from the gods. When it was over, emotion overtook me, bringing tears to my eyes.

"Ava…" Conor whispered as he lay next to me, brushing my cheek with the back of his hand as I felt my heart rate slow.

"Mmm…" Was all I could respond, making him laugh.

"Well, if we wait any longer you will fall asleep, pet." He pushed himself up. "And I can't have that…. I'm going to blow if I'm not inside you, Ava. I need you. I need to hear you scream my name while I fuck you hard." He continued, ripping open a condom and slipping it over his throbbing cock before climbing on top of me.

An urgency grew in his voice. "Look at me Ava." He commanded. I opened my eyes. "I want to see you as I slide inside you." Without waiting any longer, he showed me his now massive pulsing cock in his hand before slipping it so easily inside me, this time not stopping to let me adjust as he had the first time, but immediately thrusting hard and fast until I came back to that place of wild animalistic need. Hard and fast.

Conor fucked me like a wild man and I loved it. He wasn't soft or caring this time, but hard and commanding, taking what he wanted from my body. He gripped my wrists over my head forcefully, and grunting loud between wet licks and kisses and the filthiest talk I'd ever known. He was fucking me like an Irish god, leaving me a quivering mass of shot nerves like I had no idea what had just happened. I watched the veins in his neck throb as he exploded into me, growling my name and throwing his head back like a fucking wolf. My name on his lips was the hottest thing I'd ever heard.

Chapter 22

Belfast, Northern Ireland

Conor Murphy

I wasn't sure how long I watched her sleep. Watched her breasts rise and fall with each breath. Watched her eyelashes flutter as she dreamed. Listened to her moan delicately, as she stretched in her sleep. It enthralled me. And yet, I needed to let her go. I could not saddle such a young, innocent, beautiful creature with my dark past. She deserved more. But it would kill me to let her go.

"Ava, babe, it's time to wake up pet." I whispered to her gently.

"Mmm…oh… I don't want to." She mumbled. "No choice pet, don't want to miss that bus again." I said as I kissed her pink lips gently while circling her breasts with one finger, making her eyes open.

"Hey sexy…." Ava grinned as her hand slipped under the cover and found its way to my cock. "Look who's hard already."

"Baby, I'm always hard when you're in the room, and especially when I wake up next to you naked." She smiled at my words eagerly. "However, as much as I would have loved to wake you up by slipping inside you, it's late and you need to get moving."

Ava rolled her eyes, throwing her arm over her face.

"C'mon pet." I said as I pulled her out and off the bed. Reluctantly, she stood up, rubbing sleep from her eyes.

"Your ass is even cuter with those bruises from last night. "I commented, appreciating the pink-flushed color of her cheeks. "Now, get those skimpy little clothes back on and go back to your friends."

Ava smiled, but said nothing as she dressed.

"I'll hit the showers and meet you downstairs at the bus." I said, kissing the top of her head. I was fighting to stay casual and in control. It was even harder because she was so quiet and looking so damn sad. Despite the look on her face, I knew she would not say the thoughts that were in her head, even thought they were so bloody obvious. There was no point really. I'd told her several times that we didn't have anything more than this short time together. Stupidly, I'd thought it would be easy. As it turned out, it was anything but. And I found that I needed to repeat my own words over and over to myself.

"Okay…" She stopped at the door just before opening it. "Conor?"

"Yeah?"

"I'm really happy I met you and things happened the

way they did."

"Me too pet. Me too." I walked into the shower and heard the door close behind her.

My chest felt like lead and I struggled to breathe. The shower drowned my pain as I knew what I was headed for.

****

I kept my distance as the driver and the tour guide loaded the bus. Young people all about Ava's age were crowding around with their coffees in hand, and their sunglasses that hid their dark, hung-over eyes. They all had something in common. Something I struggled to put my finger on at first. Then it hit me. Carefree… These people were on vacation. They were young, looking for casual hookups and a good party. I hated leaving Ava with a group like this. I wanted to take care of her. What if she ended up drunk and in a bad situation again? Stop it! I scolded myself. Ava is not your problem anymore. She's a big girl and she will figure it out. These were her people, her generation. She would be fine. I was the problem. She didn't need a guy like me hanging around anymore. I had done my duty and I needed to move on and go home.

"Conor!" My head snapped up to attention at the sound of her voice calling my name.

She came running up behind me and hugged me from

the back. I turned her around and wrapped her in my arms, kissing her with everything I had.

"Please… I can't say goodbye to you, not yet…" She whispered between fervent kisses. I wanted to tell her I felt the same, and to stay and be with me forever. But I couldn't.

I gathered all my resolve and cleared my throat. "Ava, you need to go." I kissed her one more time, tasting her salty tears as they rolled down her face. I swallowed hard and my eyes began averting hers because I don't know why the fuck this was happening to me, but I was fighting back… *tears*? I felt confused and like I was two years old.

Get a grip you silly old brute. This is not you!

I heard her friends calling her from the bus. "Ava! C'mon girl, time to get on the party bus!" They called, joyful and free.

Grabbing her hand, I walked her to the bus. "Go, enjoy your trip. Have fun with your friends. You're only young once, pet." With tears running down her cheeks and her face on the verge of crumbling, I handed her over to Sam, who took her hand from mine as I turned to walk away. It was over. Time to go home.

Chapter 23

London, England

Ava Jackson

It was supposed to be the best summer of my life, but it felt like hell. Trapped inside my mind that could only think of *him*. I spent hours with my head against the glass window of the bus waiting for sleep to take me. The last few days in Ireland were the worst, though. I kept imagining I would run into him again. That some cosmic force would intervene and throw us into each other's path again. It didn't happen. Every tall, shaggy haired man I saw was him. And then it wasn't.

We finished our tour of the UK in London. I had been dreaming of going to London for a very long time. And it was everything I had imagined it would be like; sort of. Fortunately, Adriana and Sam helped to keep me occupied and mildly happy. They were by my side every minute of the day. They even made sure that one of them was always with me in the evenings when I skipped the clubbing and partying. Somehow, pub crawls had lost their appeal for me. Everything was bland, uninteresting, and immature to me.

I was good at putting on a brave face, and by the end of the UK tour, I could smile and pretend to enjoy the daily activities. But inside, it was a different story. I thought about *him* all the time. In fact, he haunted every part of me. Conor was in my head when we toured the ancient ruins of Stonehenge and walked through the city of Bath. He was there when we sat on the double-decker bus and toured the downtown London core. Even the Tower of London, a place that had fascinated me since childhood, did not live up to the expectation because thoughts of Conor clouded my mind. I imagined him standing next to me, holding my hand in his as we toured through some of the most beautiful places in Europe. I had always wanted to see these landmarks, but now suddenly, I only wanted to see them with him. Everywhere I looked, I saw him. In a crowd of people, I looked ahead, searching for shaggy hair. My head did a double take at every bearded man or tattooed arm that came across my vision. Each time, thoughts of him broke off another piece of my heart.

"Just text him Ava. You look fucking miserable." Sam said one afternoon as we stood in front of Buckingham Palace, watching the changing of the guard.

I stood in silence. Sam knew me well. She might not have approved of Conor either, but she was looking out for me. For her to tell me to text him was a big deal. "Please, I'm fine Sam." I answered, sucking in my jagged breath.

"You're not fucking fine, Ava. You smile and follow

along, but it's obvious to Adri and I that you're all broken up inside."

"Really? Adri thinks that?" I challenged her.

"Well, I didn't say she was happy about it, but yeah she sees it. I see it. Fuck, this whole tour group sees it." Sam continued.

I stared off into the distance, the sun making me squint. "He was clear it was only a fling. We both agreed. We knew it couldn't be anything more. Besides, I don't have his number even if I wanted to call him." I continued.

"Really? Because you couldn't look him up? Give me a break, Ava. I agree that it can't continue or be anything more than what it was, but maybe just message him anyway. Maybe it will help to get you some closure." Sam countered.

Not that I hadn't already thought about it. I fought with myself every day to not call or message him. But it terrified me. I already missed him so much it was painful. I hadn't even enjoyed the local cuisine because my stomach was in knots.

However, our UK tour was over. We now had two weeks on our own before we had to join up with the Italy to Greece tour. Maybe, just maybe, I could get back to Ireland during that time.

The more I thought about it the more excited I got. It wouldn't be all that bad to hop over to Dublin, then just meet the girls in Italy before the next tour, would it? It would mean missing Paris which I had always wanted to see. Or maybe... Conor would meet me in Paris! Visions of Conor and I walking down the Champs-Élysées filled my brain. Climbing to the top of the Eiffel Tower hand in hand and kissing in the moonlight on the banks of La Seine. I was becoming lost deeper into the fantasy by the second. It was crazy though, and I knew it. He wasn't the type of guy who would even want a romantic escape.

"Ava? Ava!" Someone was shaking my arm. I blinked and refocused, shaking my head free of my visions. Adriana and Sam were both next to me. The crowd that had been all around us moments ago had disappeared. How long had I been lost inside my head?

"Sorry girls... I was thinking."

"Of him, right?" Adri asked, her lips pursed and her eyes scowling at me.

"Yeah, well Sam suggested I call or message him. You know, just to help me get closure."

"Sam! Are you an idiot? She's trying to get over him! Contacting him is the absolute worst idea!" Adri shouted.

Sam just rolled her eyes. "Adri, you don't understand.

I know Ava. The more she obsesses in her mind, the worse it gets. She needs to have that awkward talk to get it through her head that she needs to move on."

I let my friends hash it out. It didn't really matter anyway. I had a plan, and I knew what I needed to do. Tonight was our last group dinner before we said goodbye to our UK tour group. I was happy that I'd caught back up with them and seen the sights with my friends, but there was unfinished business between Conor and I. I could feel it in my bones. The next two weeks were unplanned and the girls and I would take things at our pace, slowly making our way to Italy via France. I had more than enough time for a personal side trip.

"Guys it's fine. I appreciate that you both care about me. But I'll figure things out, okay?" I said, putting my arms around them both and hugging them close.

"You're going to call him, aren't you?" Adri asked, her eyes now constantly narrowed every time she looked at me.

"I'm thinking about it." I admitted "But first we need to eat dinner and say goodbye to this group." I shrugged my shoulders casually. "Let's have fun tonight. I think I need to eat something and just enjoy these moments with you guys."

"I'm watching you girl." Adriana joked, pointing at her

index finger at me. I laughed as Sam imitated her behind her back. My friends had such opposite opinions sometimes. They always kept me on my toes. I was so lucky they were my friends.

We headed back to the hotel to pack up and dress for dinner one last time. Our last dinner was at a traditional English pub, packed with locals. You could smell the fish and chips halfway down the street. My stomach needed something less oily though, so I opted for the cottage pie and a pint of Fuller's Vintage Ale. Comfort food to soothe my stomach before the text I was planning to send later that evening.

The time seemed to pass slowly. I had tried, but my heart wasn't in it. After we had finished eating, our group sat around shooting the shit and reminiscing about the last two weeks. I slipped away and went outside the pub. The silence outside was actually soothing.

It was just a text. A quick little 'hello'. A friendly chat. But, it didn't matter what I told myself. I knew why I was really doing this. I missed him. I missed him so much it felt like my insides had shattered. And worse, I was afraid that all this moping, all this sadness looming over me, meant that I was in love with him. I had only said it to myself so far, but with every acknowledgement, it grew stronger. Constantly walking around with a fake smile on my face was getting to me. I couldn't do it anymore. I couldn't fake it. I needed him. And I was sure he needed me, too.

I imagined him staring down into his beer each night after work at Eoghan's bar just feet away from where he found me. Thinking of me, the way I thought of him, and wishing I'd call. I knew he wouldn't make the first move. There seemed to be something always holding him back. Something he kept from me. Something that made him think I wouldn't want him. He'd hinted a few times that he had a dark past. Truth though, whatever it was, I knew I would get past it. He meant that much to me. After all, that's what you do for love.

So there I was, cell phone in hand, staring at his Instagram profile. It would just be a quick DM. Just to touch base. If all went well, I'd suggest more. Taking a deep breath, I typed...

Hope it's okay I msg u. Just wanted to say hey...Past 2 wks have been hard. I miss u. xo

My heart clenched up, and I began to sweat as my finger hovered over the send button. This was it. My moment of truth. Soon enough, I would know if he felt the same way I did or if everything between us had been one sided.

CASSIDY LONDON

Chapter 24

Dublin, Ireland

Conor Murphy

My phone buzzed on the bar, vibrating against my glass as it did. Someone wanted my attention. But after a full day at the jump site, I had nothing left to give. I'd been working for two weeks straight now. Nothing else since she'd left. It was the only way to keep my mind from going into dark places. Walking away from Ava Jackson at the bus stop in Belfast was one of the hardest things I'd ever done in a long time. Including fighting in Afghanistan and getting sober. In just two and a half days, Ava Jackson had left a permanent mark on my heart, and I hadn't a fucking clue how to remove it.

Again, the buzzing.

Fuck it. I turned it over and saw the words that stopped my heart. A DM request. Intrigued, I opened the app. It was… HER.

Hope it's okay I msg u. Just wanted to say hey…Past 2 wks have been hard. I miss u. xo

Suddenly it was like I could smell her, feel her skin beneath my fingers, her body soft and warm wrapped around mine. Shots of adrenaline went shooting through my veins as sweat enveloped my body. *Was I really hyperventilating?*

All I had done these past two weeks was think about *her.* I wondered if she was safe, happy, and enjoying her trip. I wondered if she ever thought of me after that tear-filled moment at the bus.

And now here she was. In my fucking phone. And she missed me.

I typed furiously, then deleted it all a minute later. I couldn't answer just yet. I needed to think about it. Think about the consequences of my actions. There was something I hadn't told her. Well, a lot actually. But there just hadn't been enough time to get into it all. Plus, telling her would have scared her away, and I had wanted to make the most of our time together.

***

Running my hand through my hair, my head dropped over and I stared at the bar in front of me. The wood was old and scratched, but Eoghan had added a coating of varnish on top for protection. At first glance, the bar was refinished nicely but when you looked closer, the scratches, the wears and tears that had accumulated over the years, were more than visible. The irony wasn't lost on me.

Eoghan called out across the bar. "Another one mate?"

"Nah… I think I'm done for the night man." I answered. I needed to walk off what I had already downed and decide how to answer Ava.

I left the bar and walked down the cobblestone street. It was the same one I had carried Ava over. Emotion hit me hard in the chest as I thought of our time together. It would be so easy to deceive her now. To never tell her. But I knew all too well that secrets don't stay secret forever.

I took a deep breath. It had to be done.

My fingers ran across the keyboard quickly.

Ava. Hope you're enjoying Europe. It was lovely meeting you but our time together could never be more than what it was. Enjoy the rest of your summer.

Send.

Fucking brutal. Pain seared through my body as I gripped my chest. Fuck, I hated myself for hurting her like that. I could see those soft caramel eyes staring at me, asking, pleading with me– *why*? The past two weeks had already been awful. But now, after having to brush her off as if she had meant nothing at all, was even worse. Being older than her would just confirm to her that my intentions were not genuine, and that she could never trust someone older than her ever again.

They say if you love someone, you sometimes have to let them go. I had never believed in such utter bullshit until now.

I checked my phone every five seconds after I sent that text. I willed my phone to buzz again. I wanted her to reach out again to ask why. To tell me I was an asshole; anything... anything at all. But there was only radio silence. Just like I knew there would be. Ava wasn't the type to question or beg for me back. She was too proud for that.

Chapter 25

London, England to Vougliameni Beach, Greece

Ava Jackson

His words cut through to my soul. I hadn't expected that response in a million years. I never expected that he would be so cold, so distant... so ruthless. Tone is a funny thing in texts. Sometimes it is bang on, and other times it's interpreted completely the wrong way. I wondered if maybe I read his message wrong. But I knew the truth. Conor Murphy had pretty much told me to fuck off.

I never went back into the pub. Sliding down the stone wall, I sat outside on the cold pavement like a homeless person, crying into my hands. My emotions were all over the place. One minute I was sobbing uncontrollably, the next, anger fired through my veins as I wanted to yell and scream at Conor. How dare he make me feel this way! Such a jerk. Then the tears hit me again because he wasn't a jerk, in fact he'd been a great man. He'd saved me from the bar, driven to Northern Ireland to help me find the bus, and even booked a stay at the hotel to spend additional time with me for one more night. All for a girl he'd known for only forty-eight hours. He was caring and sweet as much as he was intense and dangerous. He was the reason I felt shocked as if there was an electric charge in the air every time he walked in the room. He had made me feel things I hadn't thought possible, physically as much as emotionally. That's why all this hurt so much. I didn't know I would fall so hard and so fast. I was sure it was not lust. And not something I would get over anytime soon.

I was sobbing hard and uncontrollably when the girls found me. So hard that I was struggling to breathe.

"Fuck Ava! What happened?" Adriana cried, running towards me and crouching down next to my crumpled little body.

"Are you hurt? What happened?" She continued. I knew she was freaking out but I could barely talk. It had become a physical pain now. My body felt limp and ached for something I would never have. Something that was like a dream; a dream I now wished I hadn't had.

"Sam!" screamed Adriana. "Get over here! She's here, I found her!" Sam was on my other side in a heartbeat, brushing the hair from my face and holding my hands where I clutched my cellphone still. "Ava. Look at me." My eyes glanced over, but I could barely see from all the tears that were spilling out.

"Shit… you called him, didn't you?" Sam asked.

I handed her my phone and mumbled something about a DM. Sam and Adri crouched on the pavement next to me to read what I had written, and Conor's response. They were quiet after that, but both sat on either side of me and hugged me hard. I sobbed into their shoulders while they rubbed my back quietly. There was nothing to say. It was over pretty much before it had even begun. I felt, as though in just one moment, my life as I knew it had ended. Old Ava was gone. *Dead.*

***

After all the heartache I had gone through with Ryan and Ashton, it had convinced me I had already experienced everything a broken heart could take. I had been WRONG. Somehow, as fast as I had free fallen from the plane, I had fallen for Conor. In such a short amount of time, I had gone from feeling I was at the highest peak of Mount Everest to the lowest depths of the ocean.

My friends were my saviors, though. I knew it could not have been easy to deal with a party pooper during one of the greatest highlights of our lives. I was ruining this special trip for my two best friends. All because of a guy I had just met. All because of a guy who had connected with me more than anyone ever did in my entire life. *Did I just imagine it all? Was this what it was like to fuck an older man? How could he forget and disconnect with me in a blink of an eye? Was I too young still to understand the concept of a one or two-night stand?* The questions continued their torment inside me.

After we parted ways with the UK tour group, we spent a few days in London. Shopping and wine therapy are a real thing. Standing in a trendy little shop on Regent Street, Adriana encouraged me to buy a pair of insanely expensive pants. "They look incredible on you my friend. You deserve them."

"I can't afford them, Adri." I grumbled. "I'm already running low on cash."

"Here, use my credit card." She said, stuffing her AMEX into my hand.

I stared at her, slightly shocked. "Your dad gave you that for emergencies only, Adriana."

"Well, this is an emergency. You feel like shit and I'm your friend. So they're "Emergency Pants." Buy them." She commanded.

I laughed. "Can't argue with Emergency Pants."

The next two weeks went by in a haze. The girls and I traveled to France and spent most of our time in Paris before taking the train through Germany and Switzerland. All before heading down to Italy to catch our next tour group. The daytime was okay. With just the three of us, my mind stayed pretty occupied and I could enjoy the sights. Nights were very different, though. Most nights after my friends fell asleep, I

would walk the halls of our hotel, my arms wrapped

tightly around my chest trying to hold together what felt like an empty shell. I felt like the ghost haunting the hotel.

I cried alone beneath my pillow and hid behind the running water of the shower. I hoped the girls didn't notice. If they did, they didn't bring it up. There was no use. Each day that passed enabled me to have a tighter hold on my emotions. I wasn't getting over him by this point in time and I knew I never would. But I was able to hold it together better now.

Pisa, Milan, Florence and Rome. With each city, I gained more confidence in my ability to function, but the effects of such a great loss were visible physically. Despite the hot sun and the great company, I felt sick. My stomach was a mess, my face looked sunken in, and the circles under my eyes were getting bigger by the day. Sam said by the time this vacation was over, I would look like I needed a vacation. Couldn't deny that she was right. Heartbreak was definitely not good for your complexion. I was missing out on possibly the best experiences of my life. The hottest men I would never see again. Smiles from strangers gave me no motivation to move on anytime soon. I had it bad.

The southern Europe tour was better than the first. The people were warmer, and despite being more chill, the guide was way more organized. Roberto made sure everyone was on the bus and even waited an extra fifteen minutes when necessary.

Our first day in Greece was a beach day. We had crossed over from Italy by ferry the day before. It was a Sunday and Athens was packed with people. Tourists crowded every single market and landmark. Everyone was eager to get to the beach and avoid all the craziness. We would be in that mess the next day, but for today it was all sun, sand, and swimming.

Our tour had a glass-bottom boat tour planned, with a traditional Greek Mediterranean lunch. We waited on the beach for the boat to arrive, holding all our gear for the day.

"Fuck! I'm so hot. I'm sweating standing still!" Adri complained as we waited.

"Shut up, Adriana!" Sam countered. "We're all hot, don't be such a princess!"

I would have laughed at their bickering, but while my friends argued, I stared out to the water. It was a beautiful deep azure blue. The repetitive movement of the waves was comforting. I stood there mesmerized, inhaling and trying to let nature soothe my broken soul. Suddenly, I felt something tug at my attention. I turned my head and froze. For a moment, I thought I was dreaming. But *he* kept moving closer. Long determined strides. Conor Murphy was marching across the sand in board shorts, his skin glistening in the sun. Shades covered his green eyes but his expression was unmistakable. His tattoos were unmistakable. He was coming for me. I felt my body respond before my brain. Feelings flooded my heart before I could speak. My legs shook as my breathing hitched. I felt myself starting to blackout. The emotions were just too much for me. I heard voices in the background, and then everything went dark.

"Ava?" Came Adriana's voice somewhere in the distance.

"Holy shit…it's Conor fucking Murphy!" And the voices trailed away.

CASSIDY LONDON

Chapter 26

Vougliameni Beach, Greece

Conor Murphy

In the last few weeks I had tried to forget her, but it had been no use. She haunted my dreams. My mind was consumed with memories of her twisted underneath me. Her hot, wet mouth submitted to my tongue, the curves of her lush body warm and soft beneath my fingers. Twenty-four hours a day, I fought a losing battle. Just a momentary thought of her red hair and fiery spirit had my cock on the verge of exploding in my pants.

I didn't have a fucking clue how she'd react when she would see me, but I also had no choice but to take the risk. Ever since her text, I was barely functioning. I couldn't continue like this any longer. Eoghan, the guys at work, everyone had told me I needed to find her and make it right. I'd been an ass to brush her off the way I did. I knew now. And it ate away at my heart how cruel I had been, but at the moment, cruelty was my only answer. I didn't want to hurt her, but I also couldn't imagine her saddled with my baggage.

As the days wore on into weeks, I no longer cared about doing what I had initially thought to be the right thing. I thought about her all the time. I dreamed about her. Her scent burned into my brain making me taste her sweetness under my tongue at all times. Thoughts of her consumed me day and night, not to mention the desire to claim her as my own grew stronger every day. I hadn't expected it. I'd met countless beautiful women in my time. But no one had ever captured me, mind, body and soul, like Ava Jackson.

And then, there were the nightmares. Consistent visions of her red hair as she walked into the fire that consumed her each time forced me to wake in a cold sweat to the sound of my own screams. That fire had killed my parents and little sister. And should have killed me, too. Instead, it left me alone and angry. That anger had been the beginning of the end for me. Drugs and fighting eventually took me down, but the worst of it all was the secret it left me with. The one reason it terrified me to go back to Ava. Once she knew, she may never look at me the same way again. In my dreams, I could see her walking into the fire with no idea of the danger ahead. Exactly how she would perish, if she accepted me back into her life. Providing I even had a chance. I might not after how I had responded to her. But I had to try.

****

It had been a last-minute decision to go find her in Greece. I'd called the tour company to get their itinerary and booked a flight to Athens all in under an hour. It had started after yet another evening of staring down an empty pint glass at the bar, when Eoghan told me in no uncertain terms that it was time to make a change. He was the one that suggested I track her down in person. He said after the awful text, she'd probably not respond or even if she did, she may not understand how serious I was. So there I was, marching down the beach in Vougliameni, towards the only woman I ever loved, and the one I was very aware I shouldn't.

The hot sun was shining down and warming my bare skin. It felt good to feel this dry heat after the coolness of the grey Irish skies and dark evenings in the bar. Despite the crowd and the noise, I could feel her before I even saw her.

She stood there, hair flowing in the warm breeze, pure innocence and beauty in her eyes. But a certain sadness, too. She looked worn down, almost lost inside herself. My breath felt ragged as my heart slammed hard into my ribcage. This girl was nothing like the others. My whole body knew it.

Not to mention how fucking sexy she looked. One look at her and my mind instantly traveled to visions of her luscious body. I wanted her tied naked beneath me, screaming my name and unable to move as I sucked on her delectable pussy all night long. Her bathing suit was a midnight blue and mostly sheer. A deep V in the front showed off her breasts, and the high cut bottom left bare hips showing out of the top of her tiny denim shorts. She had something shiny around her hips; body jewelry– a chain. That was so fucking hot. An ankle bracelet made of shells drew attention to her shapely legs as she shifted her feet in her sandals. I watched her ass cheeks jiggle with each movement, each shift of her hips. Her shorts were wedged into her butt crack and that alone made my cock twitch even before I could reach her. What a sight. Her breasts were visible at the right angle. The plunging neckline exposed the sides of her breasts, not leaving much to the imagination. I bet by the time I reached her, her nipples would actually be visible through that sheer fabric. I could just imagine the sight of her breasts wet in this suit. And I wasn't the only one, of that I was sure. Every man on this beach was probably thinking the exact same thing.

The second she turned her beautiful face towards me, I saw shock register in her soft caramel colored eyes. Fear, desire, and excitement simultaneously crossed her face.

"Ava!" The sound of my voice surprised me. I hadn't intended to call out, much less bark at her like that. Her friends squinted into the sunlight next to her as she stood immobile, staring back in my direction. That sexy auburn hair spilled down her back beneath a large sun hat. I couldn't wait to pick her up and hold her in my arms.

The beach was chaotic, people were everywhere, and

Ava and her group looked like they were waiting for something; an excursion perhaps. But she couldn't leave, I needed her first. Suddenly her group began to board a glass-bottom boat. Fuck. I needed to hurry. I jogged a little faster and called out to her again. "Ava!"

She removed her sunglasses. Shock registered on her beautiful face, and something else, too... pain? I squinted, trying to see better, raising my arm up to wave to her. I watched as her girlfriends took a step closer, closing in on Ava. They wrapped their arms around her.

As soon as I was within earshot, Adriana called out. "Conor Murphy, what the fuck are you doing here? You here to fuck with her head again?"

"Oh, shut up Adriana. I did no such thing, ever."

"Well, you're doing it now by showing up here." she answered coldly.

I had no time for Adriana. "I need to speak to you Ava." I said, staring only at Ava.

Her eyes filled with tears. Hesitating, she stepped closer. I had a chance.

"Baby, I'm so sorry. I was trying to do what was best for you by pushing you away, but the last few weeks have been murder. There's so much I need to tell you."

I reached out and took her hands in mine.

"Conor…" She whispered out. The sound of my name on her lips was like a symphony to my ears.

"Last call for boarding!" Called the guide on the glass-bottom boat.

"C'mon Ava, we have to go." Sam ordered as she tried to take her hands from mine.

Time stood still as we all waited for Ava's response.

"Go without me." She answered without blinking, her eyes still locked on mine.

"Not this again…" Sam whispered.

"Please…" Ava trailed off. "Please trust me. I need to hear what he has to say."

"Okay, well, this is just a day trip…" Sam began, but there was a note of warning in her voice. She looked over at Adriana for support but Adriana just rolled her eyes and boarded. "We'll be back at the hotel around dinner time. Please be there Ava." Sam finished as she leaned over and kissed Ava's cheek.

"Promise." Ava whispered, still staring at me as our hands released for a moment. I wanted to drop to my knees in the sand and thank the heavens for this chance. But instead, I held it together and stepped forward, staring out into the ocean before reaching back with one hand towards her, encouraging her to join me. When her small hand slipped into mine, my heart tumbled and flipped inside my ribcage.

CASSIDY LONDON

Chapter 27

Vougliameni Beach, Greece

Ava Jackson

From the first moment I saw him, my vision blurred and my heart scarred, forever tainted by the knowledge of his existence. Irrevocably altered by both beauty and pain. I hadn't known it at first, but from the first second I had stepped onto the bus and driven away from him, I felt like a part of me had been left behind.

Those weeks after we had been together had been brutal. But I was even more worried about what would happen after the summer was over. After the craziness of the trip was over and the girls and I went back to our real lives. The plan had been to go home, find a job, an apartment, and start my adult life. Yet after leaving Conor, I wasn't sure how I would have the motivation to do any of that when all I wanted to do was go back in time and be in his arms again.

Now here he was. On the beach in Athens, unannounced and fucking gorgeous.

He was running down the beach. His usual shaggy hair tied back behind his head stressed the hard lines of his jaw and cheekbones. His beard was fuller now than it had been a few weeks ago. It gave him a more rugged caveman look that made desire pool in the depths of my belly. Muscles gleamed in the sun, emerald eyes that bore into my soul commanding me to follow glinted with reflections. That V shape that descended into his low hung shorts made me quiver at the thought of caressing him and tracing that V all the way down. Letting my hands slip beneath his shorts. I wanted to jump into his arms and ask questions later. But my heart needed me to proceed with caution.

As much as I had made insane efforts to move forward and forget him, I hadn't succeeded. I don't even think I had wanted to. Conor Murphy had made me feel like a woman, yes. My body craved his touch, but his seduction had been more than just physical. It had been emotional, too. Logically, I knew it was crazy. We had spent barely any time together, yet my entire mind and soul knew I was his.

He called my name, the sound of his voice flooding my ears and my brain, setting off a battleground inside me. I wanted to run to him but it terrified me. So many questions arose. *Why was he here? How did he find me? Or was this coincidental?*

I had barely recovered from the last time. *What if I couldn't after a second time around?*

Yet, the other side to all this turmoil was simple. *Go to him. Just go. Let him hold you in his arms. It will all be figured out.* That was the voice I listened to.

As we walked away from my friends, hand in hand, I looked up at him and smiled tentatively. His green eyes danced happily at mine. We exchanged no words for quite a while. We just continued moving down the beach away from the crowds. The warmth emanating from his body seemed stronger than the sun, and I soaked in this quiet moment of peace. Finally, the beach cleared a little, and he spoke.

"Come, let's sit and talk, Ava." His voice filled with emotion. We took a few more steps towards the water and sat down on the warm sand as gentle waves lapped at our feet. Conor wrapped a broad arm around my shoulders and pulled me into his embrace. The scent of him enveloped me, making me feel drunk and giddy.

"Babe, I apologize for surprising you like this. Thank you for coming with me.

"I'm just so confused, Conor. You were so brutal in your brush-off, yet here you are like nothing happened." He took a deep breath, but I wasn't finished. "I'm giving you a chance to explain, but I'm begging you not to hurt me. I've barely made it through the last three weeks and I can't start over again. I'm not sure I would survive another round like that."

"Ava… you mean everything to me. Despite all the reasons I know I should have walked away and never looked back, there's something about you that is not letting me do that."

Conor took my chin and turned it up towards him. "I'm in love with you, Ava Jackson."

His words took me by surprise. My heart went flying off the edge of the cliff it had been clinging to. But instead of the fall to its death I had been fearing, it went soaring through the clouds with wild abandon. I threw myself at him, my arms around his neck, my lips molded to his as our bodies crashed into each other. Conor grabbed me and held me tight as we rolled on the sand together. I ended up on top of him, straddling him.

"Conor, I love you too." I whispered fervently between passionate kisses.

"Get a room people!" shouted someone from the beach, momentarily jolting us both back into the reality that we were very much in public. We both stopped for a second and chuckled. "Take off your little hot shorts, pet." Conor whispered in my ear.

I stared at him. "What?"

"Get your mind out of the gutter little girl. We're going swimming." He chided me.

I left my shorts and hat on the beach and followed him into the water. "Don't go too far, I'm not a great swimmer." I said as I followed him further and further out. Suddenly, Conor turned around and scooped me into his arms as I wrapped my legs around his waist.

Kissing me hard, I felt myself relax in his embrace, desire flooding my senses. His mouth left mine and trailed down my neck, leaving tiny bites that made me squirm with need. My nipples ached to be touched, squeezed, and rolled beneath his fingers as they bobbed up and down, peaked and ready, beneath my suit over his wet chest. The waves lapped against us, hiding Conor's hands as he pulled my bathing suit roughly to the side. His fingers found their way to my aching center and slipped inside my body, making me rock my hips against the bulge in his shorts. His touch set fire to me, mind, body and soul. He slid my suit off my shoulders and down over my hips, keeping it wrapped around his wrist. With my breasts now free in the water, he turned around to make sure my back was to the beach so no one could see.

"I want you inside me Conor. Please." I begged shamelessly.

"Fuck, I've been waiting to hear you say that for weeks now, pet." Conor whispered, raspy and breathless.

I felt the tip of his cock brush against the folds of my swollen pussy before he rammed himself inside me hard and fast. It took a second for me to adjust to the size of him before relaxing and letting the feeling take over. The waves rocked us back and forth until I felt my pussy contract and squeeze him hard. That warm tingling feeling curled up inside me and threw me over the edge, screaming his name, moaning, and not giving a fuck who heard. My wet hair whipped him as I flipped my head back in ecstasy over my orgasm. Conor soon followed, gripping me hard as he emptied himself inside me, moaning "FUCK AVA!" over and over again. We stayed in the water for a while, holding each other and gently kissing and sensually rubbing and playing with each other skin to skin. Our naughty little encounter was completely hidden by the sea. The shoreline was shallow for quite the distance, so we had been out of reach from the tourists tanning on the beach.

We spent the rest of the day walking the beach, stopping to eat, and eventually retiring to Conor's room at a nearby hotel to nap. We slept wrapped in each other's arms, my heart feeling full for the first time in weeks.

When I finally woke, a heaviness covered my body, yet the light slowly encouraged me to open my eyes. "Conor?" I asked sleepily. "Yes pet, shhh… sleep baby." He cooed as his fingers traced the length of my bare arm. I smiled and breathed in the scent that was unmistakably his. He was here. I was safe. Loved.

I learned something that summer. It's not a big bang when it hits. It's slow, quiet, and steady. They say when you know, you know. I never truly understood that until Conor Murphy walked into my life. But in that moment of warmth and silence, I knew. I had fallen… hard. And I didn't care that the fallout might kill me. I wanted to be in that space where I could feel this love for one moment after the next. One more moment, however brief it was, was better than never knowing the feeling at all.

***

When the girls came back that evening, I told them that Conor would be staying. Adri just rolled her eyes, but at least both my friends were understanding.

Conor took another room in the same hotel and I stayed with him. He followed us around on the tour for the rest of the week, except for the last day when he headed out for the afternoon to sky dive over the Adriatic Sea. I had thought about joining him, but he cautioned me he needed to go alone. He said it had been too long since he had jumped and his mind was getting the better of him. I wasn't sure what he meant by that, but I knew he had his demons.

During that week together, Conor had told me his initial reasons for wanting me to move on without him. Beyond the physical distance of our home countries and the age difference, he felt his past would be too much for me. He had reluctantly spoken about his childhood, the car crash that killed his parents, his difficulties of growing up in foster care, and the fights and drug issues that had plagued him. All shit he had somehow thought was too much for me. As much as he had shared with me, I still had the distinct feeling that there was more. But I couldn't push him either; no one could push Conor Murphy. Maybe he was afraid of falling off the wagon and taking drugs again? I wasn't sure.

The only topic we hadn't touched upon during our talks was that impending moment when my summer in Europe would end. That was weighing on us both like a black cloud.

Chapter 28

Athens, Greece

Conor Murphy

I wanted this week to last forever. Everything had been perfect between us. Before this week, the longest I had gone without jumping was two days. With Ava's presence in my heart and in my bed, I found that I could get through a solid week before the nightmares and dark thoughts returned. She was an antidote to stress and addiction. But the more I worried about her leaving, the more I needed to jump. Finally, the day before she left, I had no choice. I needed to feel the rush of the wind on my face and the adrenaline in my blood. So, I left her to tour the last day of the ruins without me. I needed to clear my head and come up with a plan of how to tell her the one thing that I wanted so desperately to keep a secret. That one thing that I hadn't told her yet weighed on my mind like a rock. But everything was so good between us, I couldn't bring myself to do it. Maybe once she was back home though, I could do it. *Over the phone? No. Too cowardly.* I'd wait until I would see her again.

***

That night when we both returned, my head was clearer than it had been in weeks. But I knew I couldn't go to the airport with her. I needed to say goodbye at the hotel. It wouldn't be for long, a trip to America was inevitable now.

Pushing those difficult thoughts to the back of my mind, I focused instead on making our last night together extra special. Back at the hotel in Ireland, when I had spanked her for the first time, I'd slowly been showing her more each time we were in bed. Although a lot of it was new to her, she was always eager, willing, and of course I always made sure she was more than satisfied.

On this last night, it would be different. I'd been fantasizing about tying her up since that first day at the jump site. Securing her jump harness around her body had been so erotic. Watching her ass and her breasts be restrained and pushed tighter into new positions had been something that I had replayed in my head many times since.

My fantasies had filled my brain with images of doing the same things to her naked body. Watching her skin flush pink as I pleasured her while she pulled against her restraints, making them tighter with each movement. This was about to become more than just a fantasy.

When she came back from her day with the tour, I

was ready and waiting to introduce her to a little more of my extra-curricular interests. After preparing everything, I greeted her at the door of my hotel room, wearing only my boxers.

"Hello pet, how was your day?" I said, gathering her up in my arms and kissing her deeply.

"Mmm… babe." She smiled between kisses. Ava looked me up and down, her appreciative gaze making my cock rise to attention immediately. "It was fun but I missed you. How was your jump?" She asked.

"Actually, it was fucking incredible and just what I needed." I answered as I took her bags and set them down on the chair. "I needed to go alone, but next time you will have to join me. The jump sight was right next to the water and the sea was so blue."

"That sounds absolutely beautiful." She sighed.

"Not as beautiful as you, though. Come…" I said, gently pulling on her hand. "I prepared something for you."

"Babe, I really need a shower before anything else." She cautioned me, fluttering her lashes at the same time. I chuckled. "Thought you might say that, pet."

I opened the door to the toilet and she gasped in appreciation. A full bath with bubbles sat waiting for her.

I leaned down and began leaving a trail of kisses down the side of her neck. I loved listening to her breathing change as I touched her. From silent to little sounds of sucked in air, to finally an almost shaking sound as she grasped to maintain control.

She tried to turn and kiss me but I refused her touch. "Stand still Ava… Don't move." I said firmly, grabbing her shoulders and turning her around again.

"Uhh okay…" She sounded a little confused.

Slowly, I began to peel each item of clothing off of her body. Her shorts dropped to the floor, her tank top pulled over her head. Then, I left her standing in just her bra and panties as I walked around her, staring, drinking in her luscious body like a predator staring down its prey.

"Conor, you're making me kind of nervous…" She laughed. My answer was to unhook her bra and let it too fall to the floor. Her beautiful breasts swung as they were released, revealing diamond hard nipples pointing right at me. *Calling my name.*

I took a step closer. So close that she had no choice but to crane her neck to look up at me. Slipping one hand behind her neck and keeping her gaze locked with mine, I wrapped my fingers around one nipple and held it hard between my fingers. She winced a little but didn't move or even avert her gaze from mine.

"Too hard, pet?" I asked, making no attempt to release her.

Ava's breath hitched as she answered. "No, not at all."

"Good baby…" I answered, releasing her. She exhaled loudly.

Then, bending down to her level, I drew a line with my tongue against her hot salty skin, down her neck, between her breasts, all the way to her stomach and below her navel, stopping at the trim of her pretty lace panties. Her body shuddered as I slowly hooked my fingers around her panties and dropped them to the floor, encouraging her to step out of them.

Leading her over to the tub, I motioned for her to get in. "Get in and down on your knees Ava."

"You're not joining me?" She questioned.

"No, this is for you my sweet."

"Okay, but I'd much prefer it if you came in with me." She drawled.

"I know, but you won't be in here long, there's something I want to show you."

As I talked, I soaked up water in the sponge and let it fall over her shoulders and down her body. I loved watching her reaction to the water as it dripped down her erect nipples and slowly contoured the curves of her body before disappearing into the bubbles that rested between her legs. "Don't move Ava, let me wash you." I continued as my hand slipped between her legs.

"Babe…" I began slowly. She moaned in response, her eyes hooded with desire. "Remember the feeling of the jump harness against your body?"

Her eyes opened wide. A hint of uncertainty and recognition came over them. "Uh, yes…why?" She answered, clearly intrigued with what probably seemed to her like a random question.

"Do you remember the feeling of them tightening around your body and securing you into place? Because I do. I remember how the tighter I squeezed the ropes, the more your curves were pushed and pulled until your ass stuck out and your breasts were pushed forward so seductively." I spoke slowly, tracing the lines of an imaginary harness across her naked flesh as I spoke.

Her eyes hooded, her breathing labored, and she began shifting in her hips, becoming hyper aware of her senses once again.

"My favorites though, were the straps that went down in between your legs." Here I stopped speaking and slowly traced a line down the side of her hip, beneath her sex, and gently across the soft flesh between her ass and thigh. She sat further into her hips, trying to get me to touch her swollen pussy. "I fucking loved restraining you in that harness, but what I wanted even more… was to have you naked and tied up in my bed." I whispered, tightening my grip on the soft skin of her inner thigh.

Ava released a moan as I held her tight.

"Is that what you wanted to surprise me with tonight?" She whispered, a small smile melting across her face.

"Yes… but we should start slowly." I proceeded to soap her body and wash her gently, taking my time. Slipping between her thighs and never touching her pussy, teasing her nipples by dripping the water from the sponge over them then blowing on them and occasionally licking them. I was torturing her. My cock was so hard I was pumping it against the tub as I washed her. Observing all her curves wet was so hot I was ready to burst. I knew she wanted me to play with her. She was struggling not to play with herself right there in front of me. She was losing control with merely a little soap and water.

"Come now, I'll show you." I held her hand and

helped her out of the tub. She reached for a towel but I stopped her. "Stand still baby, let me." I dried her carefully with a white fluffy towel, taking care to ensure that every part of her skin was dry before scooping her up in my arms and walking back to the bedroom.

"So, did you bring the jump harness?" She asked, looking around the room. I had to laugh. "No pet, but I did buy some pretty rope that I think you may enjoy." I pulled it out of a nearby bag and handed it to her to hold.

"It's actually pretty soft." She remarked.

"That's because it's made of hemp. You will feel its tightness, but it shouldn't hurt you. Want to try? We'll keep it simple, alright?"

She nodded.

"Sit on your knees and put your arms behind your back, pet." I began.

"Like this?" She asked, moving into position as I nodded and spread out the rope to begin. "Umm... Conor? Can I still say Pineapple if I want to stop? Or should I keep that just for skydiving and switch fruits?" Humor flickered in her eyes as she looked over her shoulder at me.

Her words broke my focus and made me laugh so

hard it hurt. "Your call, baby." I answered with a kiss on her cheek.

"Okay, let's stick with Pineapple then, worked for me last time." She winked at me.

God, I loved this woman.

"Seriously, babe. Thank you for trusting me. Thank you for trusting me with your body and your heart."

"I've trusted you since the first time saw you, Conor Murphy." She whispered.

Holding her arms together, I proceeded to tie a beautiful design from her elbows to her wrists. When I finished, she was quiet but looked up at me with a smile. "It's tight… but I like the feeling." She whispered. "Actually, when we jumped, it was weird, but it calmed me to feel the tightness of the straps."

"I know baby…" I was unable to say more before driving my tongue into her hot wet mouth and claiming it as my fingers dipped into her already dripping wet pussy. I slid my fingers in and out a few times before circling and flicking at her swollen clit.

"Conor please…" She cried out.

"Bend over for me." Was all I said as I pushed her head into the bed, my hands running down the length of her back and digging into her ass. She was just exquisite. "Ava baby, you look so beautiful with your arms restrained like this and your pretty little cunt wet and ready for me. I'll be gentle with you later pet, but right now, I just want to bury myself inside you."

That was all the warning I gave her before ramming my cock inside her hot center. She cried out in surprise as I rocked her harder and faster until her screams went from shock to desire. Soon, her whole body began to shake and shudder. My hands went to her hair and pulled her head back as she came hard and fast. She was coming faster with less effort since we first fucked.

When she finished, I slipped out of her and lay her down next to me, kissing her gently. "Will you untie me now?" She asked.

I smiled. "Why? Does the rope hurt you?"

"No, just a little uncomfortable I guess." She answered.

"Good, tight is good, and besides Ava... unless you say your safe word, the rope will stay on until I decide to remove it." I stopped and waited. She didn't move or speak. "Anything you want to say?" I asked.

Ava smiled wide as she bit her lower lip seductively and shook her head.

"Then this is only the beginning of the evening, baby." I answered as I pulled her warm naked body back into my arms.

CASSIDY LONDON

Chapter 29

New York, U.S.A

Ava Jackson

Sex with Conor was an out-of-body experience. This man took everything I thought I knew about pleasure and turned it upside down. Every time he touched me, he ignited a desire in me stronger than the last time. Just thinking about what we had done together made my body crave his touch. He took his time, he teased, he was rough, and he was loving. Every time with him was a new experience. Being with an older, much more experienced man, certainly had its advantages.

The night before we left, Conor had made love to me one last time. We hadn't talked about what would happen, but he insisted that I call him as soon as we touched down on American soil. Every time I had asked him, he touched my lips and repeated the same words. "This is not over, Ava. I won't live without you."

I would have stayed had he asked, but he insisted that I go home. I knew he'd been neglecting his business by being away for so long. He was eager to get home and I couldn't blame him for that. I could only hope it wouldn't be too long before we saw each other again.

My dad picked us up at JFK and I have to admit that I was glad he did. I'd missed him, even without knowing it. Adri and Sam were staying with us the night before taking the train to their own hometowns.

"Mr. Jackson, thank you so much for letting us crash at your place tonight!" Sam said, hugging my dad hard.

"It's my pleasure to have you both." My dad smiled as he put our luggage in the car. He'd always gotten along well with my friends.

He took us out for a delicious Italian dinner and listened to us giggle and tell stories about our trip. He looked at the pictures on our phones, and genuinely looked interested. I had warned the girls not to mention Conor, though. After that awful aggressive conversation back in Ireland, I really didn't want to bring him up again to my dad. He also had no idea how much older Conor was.

Everything was going well until we refilled our wine glasses and got too comfortable. Even I had unknowingly let my guard down.

"Ava, did you text Conor when we landed?" Sam asked.

"You know it." I giggled. "All good. He's happy we got home safe." I continued, taking another swig of my wine.

Everything went silent.

"Ava?" My dad's voice questioned immediately. "Conor?" He thundered. "Not that guy from Ireland… correct?"

I stared at my dad. Sam's hand flew to her mouth, horrified that she had brought it up.

"Conor? The guy who drove you to the bus?" My father growled out. "Ava, I know you are an adult, but you still need to be careful. You were lucky you weren't hurt, staying overnight with a man you didn't know."

"Dad, you don't understand." I began.

"Of course I do, Ava. I wasn't born yesterday. But anyway, you're home now and that's over."

"Actually Dad…" I had no choice but to tell him now. Conor and I were meant to be together and I couldn't hide it any longer.

"He came to see me in Greece. We spent the week together. I love him, dad." It all came blurting out uncontrollably.

Sam and Adriana looked at each other with big eyes. "We're going to the little girls' room." They blurted out. "Be back soon!" They quickly made an exit to give us a chance to speak privately.

My dad and I stared each other down without saying

a word. Time seemed to stand still until my dad spoke.

"Ava, after we spoke in Ireland, I looked him up."

"You did what?" I yelled.

"I had to. I needed to know. And honestly, you should have as well. Do you know who he is? Did he tell you about himself? His past?"

"Yeah, I know things. He had a tough life. But what does that have to do with anything?" I answered, still miffed that my father was checking up on me and the people I met.

"Ava, I'm worried about you, baby. You're too trusting." My dad's eyes filled with unshed tears. "I've been through a lot in my life and I don't want to see you get hurt the way I was. Please, I need you to listen to what I'm about to tell you."

"Dad, if it's about Conor, I'm not interested. It's not because he's foreign or older that it won't work. And, it's not because your marriage to mom didn't work out that my life won't either."

"You're right Ava, it's not because of any of those things!" Screamed my dad, red in the face and furious as hell. He yelled so loud his voice shook. "It's because Conor Murphy is a fucking convicted murderer!"

My dad's words resonated off the walls of the restaurant. My heart lurched up and lodged in my

246

throat. I felt bile coming up. I wanted to run but my legs were glued to the floor forcing me to listen.

"WHAT?" I croaked out.

"Honey look, see for yourself…" He said, showing me his phone. "My friend Rob, you know, the private investigator?" He said more gently now, his hand on my arm. "I asked him to do some digging, and this is what he found." My dad continued as my friends returned and looked over my shoulder at the small screen with me.

The title of the article was as clear as day.

Ex-Military Sergeant Conor Murphy convicted of murder by strangulation.

"He fucking strangled a man to death, Ava! You cannot communicate with him ever again, do you understand me? Ever!"

"Excuse me–" I mumbled as I ran to the bathroom, cupping my mouth in my hands, bile backing up in my throat.

Tears blurred my vision. My brain, my heart, my entire being was on the verge of a complete breakdown. I slammed the door of the stall behind me.

"Ava?" I could hear my friends calling my name. "Ava?" they called again. But I couldn't respond. My body was revolting against this horrific news.

Then, in-between vomiting an expensive dinner into the toilet, I felt my phone vibrating in my pocket. Finally, the sickness had stopped long enough that I grabbed my phone and stared at it. It was Conor.

Chapter 30

Dublin, Ireland

Conor Murphy

It was happening again. That fucking reoccurring nightmare that had haunted me my entire life. Only this time, I was fully aware that I was dreaming.

The smoke clogged my lungs, piercing sounds of glass shattering rang in my ears. I fought to wake up, to release myself from the pain of reliving the crash again. As I fought my demons, I saw her in the distance. My precious Ava. Ever since I had met her, she had become part of this dream. Bile crept up into my throat. I tried to scream for her to stop, but I couldn't. Then she turned her head to look at me, blew me a kiss, and walked straight into the flames.

I awoke in a cold sweat. I knew what was wrong. It was me. I had let her walk into the flames without any warning as to the danger. She had no idea. I had let her fall in love. I had deceived her into believing I had nothing to hide. I was the fire and it was me she should have run from.

Grabbing my phone off my bedside table, I checked for messages.

Something was wrong. She had texted to say she

249

landed, but that was three days ago. She hadn't answered my texts or calls since then. A tightness had developed in my chest. I had a hard time breathing, sleeping, and even focusing on the smallest of things. *Where the fuck was she? Why was she ignoring me? Was it her dad?*

Even her friends weren't answering me. I was feeling ghosted, and had it been by anyone else, I would have shrugged it off. But it was Ava. *My Ava.*

Then suddenly, just as I was considering more serious ways to find her, my phone rang. I picked it up in seconds. "Ava?" I demanded. "Where the hell have you been, I've been trying to reach you!"

Silence filled the airwaves.

"My dad looked you up Conor... is it true what he found out? Tell me it's not."

Fuck! I should have known...

"Ava. Listen... I will tell you all about it, but I need you to trust me."

"Trust you? Why should I, Conor?!" Ava screamed into the phone. "Apparently, you're a fucking convicted murderer, but somehow you neglected to tell me that!"

"Babe, I didn't tell you because I was afraid to scare you... and also because I didn't want to saddle you with my past. This is why I felt we couldn't be together at first. It's why I brushed you off when you texted me that first time."

Silence filled the airwaves yet again.

"But is it true? Did you or did you not fucking kill a man with your bare hands on the streets of Dublin?" She whispered, her voice shaking into the phone.

I took a deep breath. "I did." I paused, waiting for her to hang up. But she didn't, so I sucked in another breath and dove into the dirty details.

"They convicted me, but…. I got off with a very mild sentence because it was self-defense and because of my impeccable military background." I paused again, waiting for her reaction. When there was none, I continued talking.

"He was a drug dealer who was convinced that I owed him money. I didn't, but he was aggressive and we quarreled. It got ugly fast. It was around the time when I was trying to get clean. I'd been working at the jump site for the old owners and was out of that lifestyle, but had gone back to the old neighborhood to meet up with a friend. Actually, it was Eoghan who came to my rescue. He testified that he knew I was clean and trying to get my life together. But yeah… when that guy pulled a knife on me, I snapped. I'd been fighting my whole life, and I'd been in the military. He took me by surprise and it was pure instinct to fight back. My PTSD maybe had something to do with it, or not. I had to fight for my life. It would have been me or him that night. And I'm not sorry that I survived."

I heard her breathing. She still wasn't saying anything, but she also hadn't hung up. So I kept talking.

"Pet, this was why I wanted you to leave and move on. I didn't want to burden you with my past. There's already too much against us. I know that. But I also know I love you. I won't give up on us... unless you tell me to. Tell me to leave you and never contact you again and I will. You have my word, Ava."

I paused and prayed. I'd never been a praying man, but in that moment, I prayed so fucking hard. Prayed she wouldn't tell me to leave her alone and never call her again. Finally, after what seemed like forever, she spoke.

"I don't know, Conor. This is a lot to take in. Truth is... I need some time. I need some time to think and process all this."

I exhaled. It could have been worse.

"Okay... but don't take too long, pet."

Chapter 31

New York, U.S.A

Ava Jackson

Hearing Conor's voice and his truth had been overwhelming. Before that moment, I didn't even know where our relationship was going. He had insisted that we would see each other again, but we had no firm plans. A part of me wondered if maybe there wasn't even anything to think about. Yet… he had freaked out when I didn't answer him for three days. *So maybe we had something?* Things had been so easy in Greece. I wished we could have stayed in that bubble forever.

I'd called the girls, but only to update them. Adriana had told me to cut him off and be done with him, but Sam as usual, was more understanding. She understood my dilemma and although she wouldn't have thought twice about it, she knew me well and was supportive of my process.

Then there was my dad. He was in full-blown protector mode and had cancelled my phone plan, changed my phone, and was trying his best to make me untraceable. I let him. I needed the time. I thought about Conor all day long, but I didn't have the courage to talk to him yet. I could deal with a recovering addict, but I wasn't sure I could live with an ex-con with the title of 'murderer' on his file. Even if it had been in self-defense.

Finally, I shut everyone out so I could attempt to clear my mind. I didn't need everyone saying the same things that were already in my head.

But in spite of everything that should have made me doubt Conor, I also had my personal experience with him that said otherwise.

***

I spent my days walking the city and people watching. Being alone seemed to help me focus on my own thoughts without distraction. Finally, after about a week, I felt like I was coming to a decision I could live with.

"Ava!" Called my dad as I walked in the door after yet another long walk around the city.

"Yeah, here dad."

"Here... I got you a new phone." My dad looked sheepish. "I know you are a grown woman and can take care of yourself, but... well, you'll always be my little girl."

"Thanks Dad." I smiled and gave him a hug.

"Also... there's someone here to see you." My dad

continued, his voice somewhat strained.

I looked at my dad suspiciously. "Is it Sam? Adriana?" I asked.

My dad just rolled his eyes and raised his hands up in surrender. What the hell did that mean?

I walked into my kitchen and nearly had a heart attack. Conor was sitting there casually with an arm on the back of the chair. His tight white t-shirt pulled tight across his chest. Green eyes twinkled with mischief. My heart fluttered at the sight of him. I wanted to run and jump into his arms, but I also wanted to turn and run right back out that front door.

"Conor!" I breathed, and then looked straight at my dad, wide eyed with shock.

"Believe me, I don't support this." My dad shook his head. "But I also don't want to lose you, Ava. And I have a feeling that if I control the situation here, that's exactly what might happen. So I'm hoping that you make the right decision."

Conor stood up.

"Ava… I came here because I cannot wait any longer. Every minute without you is killing me. I'm thankful that your dad even listened…" Conor paused and looked at my dad. "I showed him my file, so he knows what I've said is true."

"I still don't like it. I still think this is a mistake." My dad said coldly.

"And he's probably right, pet… on paper, everything is against us. You should take one look at everything I am and run. If I was your dad, I would definitely not want you with a man like me. But that's not the case. I'm so fucking in love with you, Ava Jackson. And if that's a mistake, then it's the best damn mistake I've ever made." Conor paused and stepped forward, just close enough to reach out and touch my cheek. His fingers skimmed the side of my face, making me flush and burn all over my body.

"This is all you babe. Say the words and I'll leave you alone forever. But I need to know how you feel."

"How I feel?" I repeated. "It was only after freefalling out of that plane that I understood what had happened the second I first saw you. It was like floating into an alternate universe, and I haven't been the same since. It was immediate and life-changing. Every time I've been away from you, I've craved you even more. I love you Conor, and nothing will ever change that."

I barely had the words out when he picked me up and swung me around the room. Everything melted away as his kiss sealed us together. The adrenaline rush of his touch, his love, and everything in-between came rushing through me like a high-speed wind. Finally, Conor set me down and looked over at my dad who had stepped off into the corner, but still had that cold, hard stare on his face. His arms were crossed disapprovingly. There was no way his opinion of Conor had changed.

"Mr. Jackson. I respect your need to keep Ava safe. However, know I will spend the rest of my life proving that this relationship your daughter and I have developed is real. And it will be lasting. I am a man of honor and integrity. I have a focus in life. My world is now Ava. I can only hope you can agree or accept it, Sir."

My dad didn't answer. He just walked towards Conor and stared him down. "You get one chance only, Murphy."

My heart flipped with joy. The last thing I had wanted was to have to choose between them. I stepped forward and hugged him hard. "Dad… I love you for believing in me and trusting me." I said as I kissed his cheek before stepping back and turning to Conor, who immediately pulled me in to his body and held me close.

"Conor you are my everything. When I'm with you, all my doubts disappear. The life you lived made you who you are and I love everything about you."

"Pet…" He said. His hands were in my hair and he nuzzled my neck. "I've waited my whole life for you.

You are a part of me."

Just like when I jumped tandem with him, Conor's words in my ears melted every fear. And now I knew that being with him was exactly where I was supposed to be. In skydiving, just like in love, everything beautiful in life is on the other side of fear.

The End

Please take a moment to review this book so that others can enjoy it too!

Dear Reader,

Thank you so much for picking up this book, it truly means the world to me. If you enjoyed Ava's story, I know that you will love Adriana's!

A small excerpt of LAYOVER (International Love Book 2) is included for you in the next few pages.

Happy Reading!

Cassidy xo

CASSIDY LONDON

LAYOVER

(International Love Book 2)

Prologue

Tristano Ricci

Baltimore, Maryland

10 years earlier…

My cock stirred at the sight of her. She was at the desk again, leaning over the fucking copy machine with her ass pushed out seductively in my direction. I wonder if she had any idea how much her presence affected me? Probably not. And that was the thing. She shouldn't have been on my radar… I shouldn't even have been looking at her. I could get kicked out of pilot training for shit like this. Plus, her father owning the school didn't help matters. He was always around, hovering over his daughter like a helicopter. As if he knew he needed to protect her. He was right.

I was only twenty-five hours away from having logged all my required practice time. I'd be done within the week and be out of here, ready to work. The past few years of studying and flying had me itching to start my first contract. Now, here I was with only twenty–five hours to go, and I found myself dragging them out just to see her. *Adriana.*

Adriana was not your typical girl. Despite her innocent aura, she had the luscious curves of a woman and warm brown eyes that made me melt. She was shy yet confident in her job. Pleasant and professional, yet slightly removed in a way that made me itch to know what she kept hidden beneath her mask.

I knew it was wrong, but every day I wanted her more. A forbidden temptation constantly clawing at my self-control. I needed to finish these hours and get the hell out of here before I did something that could make me lose everything I had worked so hard for.

Adriana Acosta

Baltimore, Maryland

10 years earlier…

My heart thumped wildly out of control. *Could he hear it? Did he notice the red welts creeping across my chest and my loud, erratic breathing?* I flipped my hair. Fluttered my eyelashes. I tried to look coy, or shy, or was it flirty? *What the fuck had they said in last month's issue of Cosmo?*

It was useless. My almost eighteen-year-old self couldn't even get a sideways glance out of him. Every day that summer, he waltzed into my father's flight school to log his hours. There were plenty of brand-new pilots just like him. But none as devastatingly handsome as Tristano Ricci. With his dark hair, olive skin tone, and bone structure that could cut glass, he was the kind of man that always stood out in a crowd. The sun shone on him and reflected back even brighter. His physique looked more like that of a fighter than a pilot. With all the hours he logged, I wondered when he found time to go to the gym. But I wasn't complaining. I did need to keep my lustful thoughts to myself, though. Tristano Ricci was god-like in my brain, and I was nothing more than a teenage receptionist to him. If even that. He was ten years my senior and starting out on a lucrative career that would take him around the world. He was not going to be distracted by a kid still in high school. At least that was my impression, at first.

Until the day that everything changed.

The day that Tristano Ricci ruined me for all other men.

It was a Thursday evening after hours, and Tristano was messing around with the planes. My father had asked me to let him know that we were closing soon. He needed to finish up the paperwork. Dad was a stickler for paperwork.

I paged him but he didn't answer. I looked at my dad for direction, when I received no answer back. What was the next step? I was already sweating at the thought of having to speak to *him*. But Dad was on the phone and he mouthed to me that I'd have to go out to the runway and meet him. He turned his back and continued on with his call. But not before tapping his finger to his watch several times. He made it clear to me that time was ticking.

Fuck. This meant I had to talk to Tristano in person. Which was also code for me stumbling over my words and sounding like a blubbering idiot. But I had no choice. I certainly wasn't going to ignore my father's wishes. I didn't need him yelling at me in Portuguese in front of Captain Ricci.

So off I went, trying to smooth my hair and adjust my

skirt as I walked nervously out to the runway. I found him sitting on the steps of the Cessna, staring up at the sky. His chiseled face and striking good looks were even more blinding against the backdrop of an emerging sunset.

"Umm. Excuse me?" I began, already feeling that unmistakable heat of desire simmering in my veins.

He turned and stared at me right in the eyes. His gaze held me captive until his voice broke the silence between us.

"Adriana," he said, rolling his R's which reflected his Italian heritage. "To what do I owe this pleasure?" Tristano stood up from his spot and casually moved closer to me, hands in his pockets, a cool professional smile on his face. His massive width and imposing height invaded my personal space and forced me to look up at him despite squinting into the sunset.

"Umm… I uhh… we called you. I mean paged you, but I guess you didn't hear. We're closing in five minutes. You need to pack up and turn in your flight log."

"Of course," he responded instantly before abruptly turning away.

I sighed. *He'll never notice me.* I turned to walk away, feeling once again defeated and invisible. It was impossible to get away without making a scene, though. Somehow, I managed to trip on a rock and felt myself tumble without warning. There was an instant between when the graveled dirt should have come up and hit me square in the face, and when I first felt the strong, warm touch of his arms around my body. Like a slow-motion video, I felt suspended in time, watching the disaster unfold before me. Fingers then stretched across my body, holding me up and pulling me away from the ground. He spun me around with little effort, and stared deeply into my eyes. He seemed to search for something, although I wasn't too sure what. I felt intoxicated by his touch, his gaze, the smell of his cologne.

"Are you hurt?" His worried eyes scanned me up and down.

"No, I'm fine, just uhhh…" I didn't even know what to say. Tristano's fingers grazed my cheek as he gently pushed an errant strand of hair back behind my ear, letting his fingers linger there for just a moment. His simple touch immediately sent waves of tingles across my body, awakening it to its full potential.

I felt myself look up, his face now inches from my own as he lifted me up to my feet. I sucked in air trying to steady myself, but as I parted my lips to breathe, my world was irrevocably altered. Tristano's lips ever so slightly brushed up against mine. Warm, sexy, and slow, they were a deadly combination. The fire was unmistakable. Even to my inexperienced body, I understood immediately how deep a desire like this can rock one's soul. His kiss lasted just long enough to morph from gentle and sweet, to reveal lust filled passion that bubbled beneath the surface. His tongue invaded my mouth, frantically searching for something unknown as he plunged it deep. It was better than a fairy tale. It was everything first-kiss dreams are made of and then some. The moment was only made better when he pulled away from me and said the words that would be on repeat in my head for the next decade.

"I've wanted you for a long time, Adriana. I know we shouldn't, but I can't deny how I feel about you. Have dinner with me. Tonight."

CASSIDY LONDON

Chapter 1

Tristano Ricci

HND –Tokyo Airport

10 years later…

"Captain Ricci?" A woman's sultry voice filtered out from the main cabin. I turned and looked into the eyes of a beautiful blonde flight attendant that I knew all too well. As always, Sophia was making her intentions clear right from the start of the twelve-hour flight. We only had twenty-four hours in Tokyo before flying back to San Francisco. Yet, this lovely girl who I had the pleasure of seeing naked many times before, was once again letting me know how she wanted us to spend the layover.

Of course, fraternizing amongst the flight crew was strictly prohibited. However, despite the official rule, it certainly didn't mean people weren't doing it. In fact, the stricter the rules were, the more people broke them. Not the actual important ones, of course. Just the fun ones.

I prided myself on rising to Captain in just under two years as a pilot. The typical journey was much longer, but I had managed to impress my employers right from the start. Not to mention my impeccable record with the ladies. Even the CEO of Air Freedom had been across my lap several times. Not to say that it was the reason I was now Captain, but it had definitely helped.

Women both adored me and hated me. But either way, I could always get them into bed. Except for one. My special one. It didn't matter how many beautiful women I took to bed or how many corners of the world I scoured. No one seemed to live up to her. *Adriana. My Adriana.* It had been both the best and the worst summer of my life. I spent that summer at flight school, logging my hours and taking cold showers. I was twenty-five at the time and she was…well, actually I had no idea, but I did know she was still in high school.

One night I had lost control and kissed her. Ever since that moment, I'd spent a lifetime trying to find that same electric spark. I never had, though. She had been something else. Something special. And clearly, something that had never been meant for me.

"Captain Ricci?" The high-pitched drawl called out to me again.

I got up from the controls, where I had been preparing for our flight, and made my way out to the cabin. We were scheduled to fly Mr. Leahy to Tokyo for business once again. It was a regular flight for him and depending on his mood, either a hellish or manageable one for the rest of us.

"Yes Sophia?" I murmured, smirking and letting my hand slip down her back to rest comfortably just above her ass. We were alone in the cabin of Air Freedom's private jet. The rest of the crew were most likely on their way, not to mention our influential passenger would be boarding soon. It made touching Sophia intimately that much more exciting to me.

"Why don't you have dinner with me when we arrive?" Sophia drawled. "I know it's a short layover, but we could grab something at the hotel maybe?" Her casual yet suggestive words danced rings around my head. Every time I slept with Sophia, I made a promise to myself that it would be the last time. She was harboring feelings for me and it wasn't fair to continue exploiting them. Sadly, logic and good reason seemed to only be reserved for the cockpit and never where my cock was concerned. *Oh well. One more time won't kill anyone.*

"Royal Park Haneda?" I asked, just to make sure we were at the same place. Typically, the entire crew would be put up at the same hotel, but Air Freedom was known for moving their crews around. There were times when I had flown to Tokyo with Sophia and flown back without her because she had been placed on a different return flight.

She nodded and slid her tongue across her lower lip seductively.

"Meet you in the bar an hour after I check in," I responded. I had to eat anyway, I justified to myself. A quick shower and a little romp in the sack with those long legs and round ass would make me sleep deeply and ensure I was rested for the long haul back. Chuckling under my breath, I walked back into the cockpit shaking my head. Didn't matter what I had planned. I could always justify it away. I seemed to be doomed for the revolving door life anyway, so I figured I might as well enjoy it.

The clickety clack of her heels mixed with her giggles dissipated as she made her way to the back of the cabin. Sophia was beautiful and smart, but I knew from experience that she wouldn't live up to my fantasy girl. No one ever did.

Fuck. This was stupid. I had to find a way to let go of her. I was thirty-five now, and thoughts of settling down were beginning to gnaw at the dark corners of my brain. I didn't want to be alone forever. Many had tried to get me to commit, and one in particular nearly did…but in the end, I always backed out. Sometimes it felt like I was walking around with an emptiness that had been left behind. Left behind by a girl who never even got the chance to fill it.

Praise for LAYOVER:

"Cassidy London has done it again! Another book I couldn't put down. The chemistry between Tristano and Adriana is smoking! At first I was so mad at Tristano but then he totally wins you over!"

-5 STAR Amazon Review

Want to read more of Layover?

Grab an eBook or paperback copy from your favorite book store today!

CASSIDY LONDON

Join Cassidy's Reader Group on Facebook:

Cassidy's Confidantes

http://bit.ly/CassidysConfidantes

CASSIDY LONDON

Acknowledgments

My crew; Betas and ARC team you are all incredible! Thank you for reading, reviewing and sharing all my books. I am so grateful to you all.

Valentine Studio Editing, your editing and support have been invaluable. Thank you for helping Freefall become what it was meant to be.

Cheryl's Literary Corner, your proofreading has been spot on. Thank you for your amazing attention to detail!

Remember readers…rules are made to be broken and steamy truths are a way of life.

Cassidy xo

CASSIDY LONDON

About the Author

Cassidy London has been in love with books ever since she can remember, particularly scandalous steamy romances. When she's not writing or reading dirty books, Cassidy can also be found masquerading as a wine drinking suburban mom in Montreal, Canada.

Printed in Great Britain
by Amazon

45681189R00158